SURVIVAL

CHRISTOPHER BROWN

authorHOUSE™

1663 LIBERTY DRIVE, SUITE 200
BLOOMINGTON, INDIANA 47403
(800) 839-8640
WWW.AUTHORHOUSE.COM

First published by AuthorHouse 11/29/05

ISBN: 1-4259-0011-9 (sc)

Printed in the United States of America
Bloomington, Indiana

This book is printed on acid-free paper.

To the memories of Dad and Pap.

I couldn't have done this without the help and support of my friends, family and, of course, God. My wife Kathleen and sister Traci were my biggest critics and this book couldn't have happened without them.

To my best friend Jeff, he helped with the initial concept and he created the cover.

TABLE OF CONTENTS

Prologue: The Bargain 1

Chapter 1: A Hard Days Night 17

Chapter 2: Surprise 30

Chapter 3: The Long Walk...45

Chapter 4: The Gathering...59

Chapter 5: Lost and Found...73

Chapter 6: A Friend...88

Chapter 7: Into the Depths 99

Chapter 8: Choices..107

Chapter 9: First Contact..119

Chapter 10: Separation Anxiety 133

Chapter 11: Desperation...143

Chapter 12: The Hunt Begins 154

Chapter 13: The List 164

Chapter 14: Best Laid Plans.......................................173

Chapter 15: Most Dangerous Game...........................183

Chapter 16: The Ties That Bind.................................195

Chapter 17: The Fatal Mistake...................................206

Chapter 18: Escape 215

Epilogue: War 234

PROLOGUE:

THE BARGAIN

They are getting less attentive by the day, he thought with a pang of distaste for those who were not capable of staying focused. He took in the large auditorium filled with this semester's crop of students. Some of them stared at him with blank stares while others blatantly placed their heads on their desks, obviously sleeping. *How do they expect to gain any sort of knowledge from me if they cannot even bother to pay attention for two short hours? These pathetic excuses for students are to be the next wave of scientists and doctors? I pity the future.* Unable to find a single student who could reach his level of acceptable intelligence, he placed his black dry erase marker on its shelf on the bottom of the large white board, let out an audible sigh and said, "OK class. That's all for today. Remember to read Gray's Anatomy The Thorax, pages one-hundred-twenty-three to one-hundred-thirty-seven for Monday."

He stood at his podium gathering up his effects, staring at the sea of uninterested faces as they scurried to escape his scrutinizing stare. He could tell that they longed for the ease of their next classes, but long ago he resigned himself to accept nothing but the best. He would not allow himself to be seen as simply adequate by allowing his students to be seen as such.

"Professor Faustus, I was hoping to talk to you about the last exam. I know I was supposed to be here, but I had an emergency that needed my attention. Is there any way that I can take a make-up exam?" the nervous student asked as he glanced at the cold, unsympathetic eyes of his professor that rested behind those thin wire-framed glasses. He knew as he asked the question that he would never be allowed to make up the exam, but his financial aid would be cancelled if he did not at least try. *Science waits for no one. If you miss an opportunity, you may miss out on your dream,* the professor often said.

Without pausing to give even the illusion of false hope, Professor Marlin Faustus glanced disapprovingly at the youth who was one of the ones resting their heads upon their desks, reveling in the fear and desperation that radiated from the young man and said snidely, "You know the rules. There are no make-up exams in my class. This class will be treated as if you were in the field working in your own laboratory and if you miss your chance out there, you cannot ask for a retry. It is not my responsibility to make life easier for you. Maybe next time you will put forth the effort to attend class."

"But sir." The student pleaded. "If you could make an exception just this once, it would help me out a lot. If I get a low score in your class, I won't be allowed back next year."

Dr. Faustus sighed and looked into the eyes of the bold student, "Do not think that I am unsympathetic to your situation, but didn't I just see you sleeping in my class?" The student stammered as he tried to come up with an excuse to cover for his actions.

Faustus raised a hand to stop any further embarrassment that the student might bring upon himself and said, "There really is no arguing here. Had you bothered to pay attention I might have considered it, but your complete disrespect for my class just shows me that you are not meant to be here. Now, I must be going. Good day."

The young man hung his head, accepted his defeat and mumbled unintelligibly. As the demoralized student walked away he thought that maybe he was not quite cut out for this life after all.

Dr. Faustus glared at the youth as he slinked out of his classroom taking the long walk up the large center stairway that lead to the hall doors, constantly wondering how people like him were ever going to get by in society. The professor had decided long ago that those who were not truly committed to science did not deserve the knowledge that he imparted. *And after all, science is the only real thing that you can count on.*

Without further interruption from the other students, Faustus gathered his lecture notes from the podium, placed them in his worn briefcase and headed to his office, which was actually a moderately sized room with enough space for his desk, a small table and a few shelves. Dark stained floors and worn carpets were some of the more attractive elements in his workspace. However, Dr. Faustus barely even noticed these, after all, physical comforts were not important to him. All that mattered was his work.

Towards the back of the room away from the lone dingy window with its blind constantly drawn was where the lab equipment dominated the area. Various beakers filled with liquid colored every hue of the rainbow lined the back wall and each were named in such a way to suggest that the good doctor had read entirely too many stories as a child. Belling the cat, The Bee and Jupiter, but by far his favorite, and the one he would spend his most time with, was The Philosopher's Stone.

The Philosopher's Stone was to be his greatest achievement. It was more than a mere experiment. It was a promise he made long ago. It was to be his gift to mankind. A cure for everything. Preliminary trials proved to be problematic at best with results ranging from a temporary remission to amplification of the disease. However, no matter how he tried, he could not get the chemical to bond with the cells in order to protect them from disease.

He sat in his dimly lit office alone and reflected upon his past attempts to administer his cure to some blood he had infected with a flu virus. He thought of the times that he was so close to completion and the other times that he was far from victory. With a furrowed brow, he thought of how one of the tests had met with disastrous results and had caused him to postpone his experiments on living things.

He had introduced a new mixture of the Philosopher's Stone to blood cultured with the common cold. The results were swift. It had simply exploded; sending tiny shards of the test slide it was placed on in every direction. It seemed that once the white blood cells came in contact with the agent, they would vibrate at such a speed as to induce instantaneous combustion. While the test was not done to a living being, his new microscope was destroyed.

"I have this great discovery in my hands but it is not yet complete." he said to himself as he sat in his lonely office surrounded by books that seemed to offer no answers to his myriad of questions that he continued to ask them. "I have tried for many years to find the correct combination of chemicals that will produce my cure, but there is nothing that seems to be able to hold it together once it enters the bloodstream."

He leaned back in his threadbare office chair as he read over his notes once again looking for the missing piece, the hours passed like minutes and he eventually sank into a deep sleep with his head resting on his journals.

Six months have passed since that day. It was finally summer break and Professor Faustus had just finished with his latest class of disappointing students and began walking back to his office determined to continue his work. On the way he began muttering to himself about the lack of focus among today's youth and realized that this crop of students was even lazier than the last. He noted that they had no drive for the search and he scoffed at their blank stares as he discussed the most basic of theories. *They take no joy in the simple discoveries,* he mused as he passed by a group of his students. *All they want is to read the books and absorb their knowledge without having to earn it themselves. They may have given up on true science but I won't. Not when I am so close.*

He entered through the door and walked past his tiny desk with its simple banker's lamp that rested behind his stack of notes and term papers that begged to be graded. Dismissing the works of those he saw as not only inferiors, but also unworthy of his time, Faustus ignored their papers and instead sat at his lab table and reflected upon the past few months and his trials of the latest experiments. At how in the latest experiments, the results were improving. The cure was becoming more and more stable with every new synthesis of the formula.

His heart was full of both triumph and disappointment at the results of his tests. There were still samples of the original vaccine lining the shelves. He had to synthesize more of the Philosopher's Stone on more than one occasion, and he remembered the mixture so well that he no longer needed his notes. He was confident enough to mix it without even glancing at his report. He knew how it would react with virtually every chemical in his office and a few that he had to get from friends in outside sources. He knew that his theories had merit and that they would work, but he was running out of money. His savings account was nearly dry, the university was beginning to ask questions about why he needed so many materials and the bank would not allow him to mortgage his home yet again.

His brow furrowed in disgust at just how close he had come to finding his answer, to finding his truth. *At least it held for a short time. It was more successful than I had expected. Just so much time has passed. When will I find what I need? Maybe it is time to show them. Maybe they will give me the proper funding I need to get all of the supplies to reach my cure. Yes, the time is now. The world must be saved.*

These thoughts echoed in his tired brain as he finished up his log for the day, carefully noting every detail of his experiment. He wanted to leave nothing out so that he never repeated the same experiment twice. To do so was seen as a failure. To repeat mistakes was unacceptable.

Determined, Faustus picked up his phone and called the office of the Dean and arranged a meeting of the Board for the next afternoon. Once that little detail was taken care of he proceeded to go through his routine of recording the day. After he finished logging his events in his journal for the day, he walked out of his office looking forward to what tomorrow would bring. "The Board will see what I have done and they will have to give me the funds I need." he said cheerily to himself as he headed for his home. He realized that for the first time in years, he was truly happy.

Out of the shadows of one corner of Professor Faustus' office stepped a shadowed figure. "Interesting." was all that was said as he picked up the report left on the desk and thumbed through the pages. "This may be the one that I need to complete my work. He could be my catalyst." Just as quickly as he stepped into the light, he was gone.

Daybreak brought with it a renewed sense of hope and accomplishment. Faustus was so caught up in his thoughts that he barely noticed the time.

"I must get to my office. The Board must be made aware of my miracle today, " Faustus said as he gathered his things to prepare for what should be an easy meeting. *After all, who would not want to give mankind their cure?* The speech he had prepared for this day ran through his mind like a sonnet. He had chosen just the right words that would convince them all of not only his intellect, but also the nearness of his vision.

He entered his office and gathered his reports and notes prepared for this occasion. As he was leaving, a student entered and began to ask about the next semester's schedule. "I really cannot stay and discuss it right now. I have an important meeting I must attend to." he said as he pushed past the annoying student and rushed off to secure his destiny.

Running to the copy room and cursing the bothersome student as he went, he feared he was going to be late. He had planned for enough time to do everything, but what if there was someone at the machine? Did he want to explain what his vision was before he got the Board's approval? Thankfully, the room was empty and he even had enough time to run a few extra sets off just in case one of the members lost theirs.

Johnson never was all that reliable.; he thought absently as he collected the documents and placed them in individually labeled manila envelopes. As he sealed each of them his excitement for the chance to gain acceptance for his work began to increase. He looked at the beige envelopes that contained his life's work and said, to no one in particular, "All your life you work for a dream and then one day it happens. It finally arrives. Today is our day Mother. I may not have been able to save you, but I can give you your wish and save others."

The meeting lasted the better part of five minutes. One of the elder members, Dickens his name was, was the first to speak up after reading the report. Dickens glared in utter confusion at Faustus and practically screamed, "What in God's name are you thinking man? Did you really think that you could just walk in here and expect us to fund your little fairy tale?"

"Fairy tale!" Faustus exploded with righteous indignation. "This is science my dear friend, not fiction. I have here proof that my cure will work once I obtain the proper materials."

Marla Jenkins, her long, silver hair held behind her reading classes, interrupted him with a scolding look upon her weathered face and said with a tone of voice that would accept no arguments, "This is impossible. There are no such things as cure all pills. How can you as a scientist believe that such nonsense exists? I thought that this type of thinking went out with the snake oil salesman. Is that how you see yourself *doctor*?" The last word said with more than a hint of sarcasm and accusation.

"What madness are you speaking woman? I am not talking of fleecing peasants out of a few pennies; I am talking about the end of all illness in the world. Surely even someone as short-sighted as yourself can appreciate what I am trying to accomplish." the professor snapped at he glared at the entire board. "How can all of you be so closed minded on this subject? Surely you must want to be able to rid this world of the horrible plagues that it contains!"

Dickens again spoke up, "Of course we do, however, we want to use real science and not stories better left to…"

"You closed-minded cretin," Faustus jumped in, not even allowing the sentence to be completed, "This *is* real science! If you would look at page thirteen of your packets, you will see that I have had…"

"That is quite enough!" the Chairman, David Roberts, rose like a king addressing his assembly and said, "This matter is closed for discussion. We will not be a party to this drivel. Now Marlin, this is not the only piece of disturbing news that has been brought to our attention. There is also the matter of microscopes."

Faustus fidgeted nervously because this was the one thing he feared the most. They had found out how he had been funding his experiments.

"Recently." David continued. "Our accountants have brought us requisition forms for new microscopes for your lab classes. However, they can't seem to find these microscopes. After a thorough search of your lab, none of them could be found."

"I can explain." Faustus stammered, sweating profusely.

"There is no reason to explain." David cut in calmly. "It is abundantly clear what happened to the money. You do realize that misappropriating finds is a very serious offense. If you will be willing to submit yourself to a psychiatric exam, we will work with you to make sure that you stay out of jail."

"Dear friend I am not crazy!" Faustus said, practically livid with rage. *How can they behave like this? The sheer magnitude of a cure like this is staggering and they talk about me like I am insane! Do they not see the good we can accomplish?*

With a heavy sigh the Chairman spoke again and said something that left the Professor in a stunned silence for the first time in his life, "Marlin, I am only looking to help you. You have been an excellent professor and a good friend, but if you will not work with me, then I am afraid we will have no choice but to revoke your tenure. You will clean out your office immediately and be off campus by the end of the day. Security will be by to make sure you comply. If you refuse to leave the campus you will be arrested. We hope you will cooperate and not embarrass this fine institution any further."

"But," he started to protest, staggered by the casual and quick dismissal of his ideas by the Board.

"No buts Professor. We cannot allow this type of behavior to go on in our school. Why the lawsuits from the parents alone would bankrupt us. How would it look to have a school with a tradition of elegance such as ours showing support for a madman with delusions of grandeur? Really Marlin, surely you can see our position on this. We will also be reviewing your past requisitions to see what else you have claimed to have ordered. This meeting is adjourned."

As the Chairman finished speaking he simply stood looking down at the professor like a parent that had just admonished a spoiled child and they all walked out of the room talking amongst themselves and ignoring the pleading explanations of Professor Faustus.

The walk to his office was a long and lonely one filled with confused thoughts and anger. *How could they? They are trying to destroy my dream. I am so close to helping everyone and they are willing to throw it all away over a simple thing like fear.* He allowed himself a brief moment of pure anger as he slammed his foot into a garbage can and sent it all of five feet. The good professor may have been brilliant, but he was not very athletic.

Nursing a sore foot, he straightened his thin tie, adjusted his tweed coat, and hobbled to his office to begin the agonizing process of removing his things. Along the way his thoughts raced as he tried to decide where he was going to go from here. *I can't go to another university. Surely these short mined cretins will tell anyone willing to hire me that I am engaged in horrible experiments or some such nonsense. They have no idea what I am working on. They will never know my dream. They will not have a chance to receive my cure. That will fix them.*

When he opened the door to his office, he realized that he was about to do one of the hardest things that he had ever done. He had to dismantle his dream. He didn't have the funds to continue his research out of his home and no one would simply keep donating the supplies that he needed.

With great sadness in his heart, he had to admit to himself that his life's work was over. He could not continue the experiments any longer without the proper materials. When he finished packing the last box of lab equipment, he sighed, wiped a tear from his eye and looked around his familiar and now so empty office that served him so well over the years. "Good bye." was all that he said as he closed the door on a chapter of his life that held so much promise.

A shadow moved in the back of the Faustus' former office and a figure emerged. "This was very fortunate. Could it be that even fate wants me to complete my plans?" the figure said to the empty room. Dark eyes narrowed in deep concentration as he attempted to work out the best way to accomplish his goal. A slight grin appeared on his face that held no sense of good will as he came to a sudden realization. "I have just the person to make sure that my plans will come to fruition. I don't like to involve too many people, but the time has come to finally put everything into motion. It must be. My dream must come to pass."

Alan Salvin, president of a multi-national cosmetics company, sat at his large mahogany desk and reflected upon his life. Having never married, the aging man had no one to share these later years with him. He looked out of the window of his stately mansion at the waxing moon and casually wondered what his life would be like if he could do it again.

"No sense wondering about things you can't change old man." he said to himself as he ran his hands through his thinning, white hair with liver-spotted hands. He thought of the many wrinkles that now marked the once handsome face. More than a hint of depression seeped into the once booming voice. "You may have created one of the greatest cosmetic companies in the world, but you have never had luck with women."

He glanced back down at the clock and it read midnight, the numbers glaring from across the room. Reaching for the light switch that would shut off the small desk lamp, he noticed that he could no longer read the lighted numbers anymore. He turned the light to get a better view of the clock when a voice suddenly stopped him and made his blood turn cold. "That's far enough Mr. Salvin." came the voice from seemingly nowhere. "I have a proposition for you."

The television glowed dully in the darkened room casting a faint glow upon the miserable environment. There were things strewn about in such disorder as to make it appear as though the place had been robbed and then attacked by a tornado. However, no robbery had occurred in the modest home of Dr. Faustus and no disaster of the natural variety had occurred. He had simply lost all will to do anything ever since he was let go from the university.

He rose from his stained couch to make yet another trip to the refrigerator as was his nightly ritual. It was three weeks since he lost his job and depression had more than begun to set in, it seemed to be his best friend. After numerous rejections from high schools, pharmaceutical companies, and even a dog food plant he decided to resign to live in the filth and ruin that he felt so embodied his life.

He opened his refrigerator and noted with disgust that there were things growing in there that even he could barely identify. "I guess it is time to go shopping again." he said to himself absently. He reached in and grabbed the one item of food that was still identifiable, a slice from a pizza that he had ordered a few days ago when he was feeling particularly down about his situation. He held the pizza in his hand and simply stared at it for a moment. *Has my life really become this? Have I sunk this low?*

"Dr. Faustus," a voice from behind him bellowed. "I believe I have something to tell you."

Unable to suppress a girly little scream, Faustus stood up quickly and completely forgot about his thoughts of life and pizza. "Who…Huh…What…" was all that he managed to say as he looked with shock upon the man standing before him. Easily taller than his five foot eight frame, the doctor could only think that this was the perfect end to his miserable existence. *To be killed in my own home without ever knowing my dream, a fitting end to a failure.*

"Relax doctor," the figure said in a calming tone that seemed to reverberate through the room. "I am not here to hurt you. In fact I have a proposition that may just turn your life around. I want you to have this." A large gloved hand moved aside a set of dishes that have not been cleaned in days and on the filth-encrusted counter he placed two objects. The first was a simple business card with the company name Maverick Cosmetics embroidered in gold lettering across the front and had a phone number written on the back. The second item was a small glass vial that appeared to have a slight orange glow from the strange liquid inside.

The professor bent over and adjusted his glasses as he stared at the strange substance. "What is this?" he asked in astonishment as he examined the vial.

That was seven years ago.

CHAPTER 1:

A HARD DAYS NIGHT

The alarm clock gave its usual wake up call around 7 p.m. A tired hand slapped the snooze button in hopes for just a few more minutes of rest. Realizing that the gesture was futile, the young man rose to face what was sure to be just another boring day in a long line of boring days. He slipped into the shower to get ready for his nightly tour of duty just like he has done for the last three years. The uniform that he wore felt like it was the only piece of clothing he had in his wardrobe. Yes, the life of a security guard was a tough one, but he was willing to handle the rigors of the job as long as he was able to. The only thing that made it bearable was the fact that he shared the shift with his best friend. Well, that and the television he brought with him every night.

Granted, the work was not all that difficult. After all, how much can happen at a cosmetics testing facility anyway. Looking in the mirror by his front door he said to himself, "Well Chris, I guess it is time to make sure that the building is safe for another night. Maybe I should call in sick today."

Laughing to himself at the thought of something actually happening at the usually calm building, he placed his ever so stylish hat upon his head, grabbed his keys and headed over to pick up his partner in law enforcement.

His partner and friend was never the easiest of people to get motivated or the most enthusiastic about going to the job. Chris reached under the false rock that fooled nobody, unlocked the front door and walked into the house to get his compatriot up and ready, as was the tradition. You see Jeff was never one for alarm clocks. Granted, he did have them and even remembered to set them from time to time, but he broke them just as frequently. It seems that they all had little "accidents". Sure, there were four accidents this month already, but they say most accidents happen in the home.

Sighing, Chris walked up to the bed where his seemingly dead partner laid and proceeded to give the traditional swift kick that jolted the bed and sent a shock to Jeff's system. "ACK, I'm up! I'm up!" he said as he often did. "For God's sake man, when are you going to find a new way to wake me up? You know I'm going to have a heart attack one of these times and you will have to take care of the lobby all by yourself!"

"Oh what would I ever do?" Chris laughed placing a hand to his forehead in mock despair, "Who would watch TV with me if you failed to wake up one day? I would have to train a new sidekick. Sure I could call an ambulance to try CPR, but that is way too close to work for me." Grinning he walked out of the room barely hearing the mild grumbles of Jeff as he worked himself out of bed to prepare for another night of hard work and TV. The job of a graveyard shift security guard was a tough cross to bear.

"Hey, guess what I got today." Jeff said bubbling with excitement as he fumbled with a plastic bag. "A new video game. You think I should bring it along?"

"You didn't get another fighting game did you? I knew I should have called in sick. I wanted to." Chris asked with a more than slight look of disgust etched upon his face. The thought of playing yet another game where you simply punch and kick each other really didn't appeal to him. Wishing that Jeff would get a game that would challenge his intellect instead of his hand-eye coordination was an exercise in futility.

"Yeah, I got Ass Kickers Special Championship Edition," Jeff said while barely able to contain his excitement. "It has 3 extra costumes and one more move for each character compared to the last version. I can't wait to play."

Noticing that Jeff was lost in the glassy eyed gaze of one who just acquired a new game, Chris simply nodded and accepted the fact that he was going to spend the night listening to strange sounding moves in a language he couldn't understand.

Helping Jeff to gather the rest of the equipment and his lunch, Chris loaded the car and prepared for the pure fun and excitement that was to be this night. At least they wouldn't have to watch Andy Griffith. "OK man, time to go and get our beauty sleep." Chris said as he headed toward the door and another night of fun filled patrolling.

Ready for the trip to work, they began the long and familiar trek down the now mostly deserted streets to Maverick Cosmetics. "Damn," Chris exclaimed as he glanced at the dashboard. "I have to stop and get gas. You need anything from in here?"

"Yeah, get me a soda. You know how fighting games make me thirsty."

"I guess all that exercise must get to you," Chris grinned.

The Gas and Grub parking lot was empty as it usually was at 10 p.m. They walked into the store and waved at the clerk like they have done many times before. It felt good to have a routine. They proceeded to head back to the oversized cooler holding the various beverages and pondered over their choice, even though they would simply get their usual. It was all like clockwork. Grab a soda, stop by the magazine rack and head off to the nightly grind.

"Look," Jeff said excitedly, "it's the new issue of Big Breasted Babes on Bikes! You don't have this one do you? This should complete your collection!" Jeff then broke into a hysterical laughter at Chris' expense all the while he realized that it could get him killed or at the very least severely maimed.

Chris considered smacking him into a coma but thought against it because then he would have to carry him back to the car. The idea of carrying a three-hundred-twenty-pound man across a parking lot just was not what he wanted to do tonight. That was when he noticed the one magazine he had been waiting for, Games Monthly Magazine. It was going to have new screenshots of the horror game of the year, Mission

Destruction. Guaranteed to be the shock fest that they were looking for.

They stopped by the candy section to load up on sugar filled goodness before they decided that it was time to head to work. After all, the lobby was not going to watch itself.

Chris entered the lobby and echoing throughout the area was a low and deep rumbling. The sound was practically loud enough to shake the inspirational posters off of the wall. He resigned himself to the task at hand and walked over to the guard desk to perform another one of his nightly duties. "Mike!" Chris screamed as loud as he could.

The poor gargantuan of a man screamed and leaned back on his already unsteady chair, which caused it to topple and send the obese man to a hard landing on his backside. "What in the hell is wrong with you man?" Mike gasped as he felt his chest to make sure his heart was still beating. How he was able to feel anything no one could guess. If the man were to be cut open, it was rumored that he would bleed bacon grease. To say he was unhealthy would be a terrible understatement.

"Mike, if you snored any louder the boss would have come up from downstairs to see if there was a riot going on." Chris chided barely able to hold back a grin. "I know that you may not take this job very seriously, but there are some if us that do. We believe in the responsibility that we share with our brothers in arms every night! Dedicated! Committed! Caring!"

In that instant Jeff walked through the door carrying the television and game system yelling, "I seriously can't wait to kick your ass tonight. No one can touch my mad skills!"

Mike gave a glare that would melt steel and said as he looked at the overstuffed arms of Jeff, "Dedicated huh?"

Jeff set the items down on the desk and began to go on a tirade about how great his game was and how he was going to enter a contest one day and become the Supreme Fighting Master. It was the same thing every time he got a new one of these games. Chris however quickly changed the subject in an effort to avoid the speech that was sure to come from Mike. "So isn't it about time to go home and spend some quality time with the little lady? Tell your wife I said hello. Bye-Bye…" Chris said as he walked the man toward the time clock and then to the door.

Finally Mike left the building and once his car could be seen leaving the parking lot Chris turned to Jeff and growled," You know we always wait until Mike leaves before bringing in the TV. If I didn't catch him sleeping, he would have run right down to the supervisor and ratted us out."

"Not if you would have given him your Twinkie." Jeff joked as he set up the equipment as he did every night.

"He will never touch my Twinkie. I would have killed him and sold him to science first." Chris said while he shook his fist menacingly in the air in a mock expression of rage.

Within minutes the set-up was complete. The television cast an eerie glow on the walls and the sound was turned to its usual low so that they would have plenty of time to hide it in case of a surprise inspection. Before they could enjoy their nightly ritual, they had to take care of some business first. The logs had to be reviewed, the front doors had to be checked and the rock-paper-scissors match for who took the first controller had to be played. After all, that was the lucky controller and whoever lost the first match had to make the first set of rounds.

Chris lost the game in record time and steeled himself for the long walk through the upper floors of the building.

At least I don't have to go downstairs. Saves me a bit of work and I don't have to listen to old Duncan bitching at me for some uniform violation, he thought as he grabbed the oversized monstrosity that was the Detex clock and slung it over his shoulder by the thin and ever worn leather strap. If not for this little contraption and the keys hanging on chains scattered about the building, he wouldn't have to take rounds at all. *But no,* his mind replied scornfully, *I have to take the little metal keys hanging all over this building and turn them in this clock. Then they can know that I made the rounds. It's like they don't trust me.*

Getting himself ready for the long walk through the four floors above ground, Chris began absently whistling the tunes of the oldies shows that repeated every night. He could tell you the names of all the people in Mayberry and he could tell you which episodes of "Car 54" were the best.

Walking up the first flight of stairs into the visitor's section of the building, he began to head towards the first key located near the candy machines. Sure, the machines were changed once a decade and refilled with candy from machines that had broken down, but hey, when they charge you as much as they do, how can you resist.

Winding his way through the building is something that he has become accustomed to and could do it blindfolded. Casually strolling through the cafeteria, he glanced at a few newspapers left on the table and decided to *borrow* one. Tucking it under his arm and nervously glancing around as though someone might see him committing the crime of the century, Chris headed off to the next key and the men's room it lived next to.

Back in the lobby the sounds of struggle could be heard, but just barely. Jeff held out as long as he could, but Chris was gone for about five minutes and he was eager to try his new game. Sitting back in his chair, Jeff was so focused on his game that he almost never heard the phone ring. In fact it took him three rings to answer it.

When he finally pried himself away from his entertainment and turned down the sound completely, he picked up the phone and said with a slightly annoyed voice, "Hello, Maverick Cosmetics. Front desk."

"Jeff," a perturbed voice could be heard to yell even if the handset was resting on the floor, "what took you so long to answer the damn phone?"

"Sorry Captain Corning, I was just checking the front door. I wanted to make sure that Chris locked them right this time." Jeff said as he struggled for an excuse realizing that the truth could get him fired. Sure he had no trouble making his partner sound incompetent, but if they were caught again, then this would be their third offense this year and that means termination. Not the bloody death kind, they would simply be fired, but being fired meant no money for essentials like rent, food, and videogames. Not necessarily in that order.

"Where the hell is Chris at?" the captain asked practically brewing with frustration. Jeff could picture the man sitting in his office with his tiny amount of power feeling as though he were a king. He saw that little vein about to burst that often appeared when the captain got angry. Once when he caught Mike with his hand stuck in the candy machine, Jeff thought for sure that the vein would explode. Not that he would feel terrible about it.

After all, the man was nothing more than a bully. He tended to throw it around that he could have someone fired if he wished. The captain was about as intelligent as a fire hose and as tactful as a bus hitting you in the face, but he did have one thing going for him, retirement. This was the captain's last year with the company and soon someone within the building would be promoted to captain. Jeff almost wanted the job, but realized that he would actually have to work. He made a mental note to suggest Chris for the promotion. He could see the banners now, *Vote Chris for Captain!*

"Chris is making the first round. He wanted to go first. He is very dedicated." Jeff began to explain to the captain. "Why you should have heard the speech…"

Irately Corning yelled into the receiver, "I don't care about speeches. Just make sure that you do your jobs. Last week you missed three keys and Chris missed one.

That is unacceptable. The both of you have been here for three years and you…"

Jeff had long since learned to go into a state of trance when the captain started ranting. He stared off into the distance at a picture of a runner on a sandy beach with a caption that simply said *Determination.* He then realized he had no idea what the hell it was supposed to be telling him and decided that he hated inspirational posters.

"…And that's the last time I am going to tell you," the captain finished.

"Yes sir." Jeff said in a semi-respectful tone. *Just a few more months and he will be gone,* Jeff kept repeating to himself every time that the captain went on a tirade. It became a mantra of sorts.

Jeff sat back in his large leather chair, the only luxury that the company provided, and began to think of the days to come when the captain will no longer be able to make his ears bleed with his screaming. Were he paying attention, Jeff would have noticed the woman enter the lobby.

"Hello Jeff." she called from the front door giving him no time to place the contraband television under the desk.

"Hey Janet." Jeff said with all the effort he could to not let her know how nervous he was.

Janet was a scientist and on the top of her game. She was hired shortly after Jeff and Chris had been assigned to Maverick Cosmetics. While incredibly brilliant in the lab, she was somewhat lacking in the sense of direction department. The guys, mainly Jeff, had to show her around the building on more than one occasion. She was also the nicest person you could meet and they never had to worry about her telling anyone of their late night tournaments.

"In for another 10 hours Jeff?" she asked with a wide grin. "How will you pass the time?"

"Oh, I'll manage." Jeff replied placing his game controller on the desk. "Want to take a shot at the title?"

"What are you talking about? I took that from you last week." she said mockingly. "You know you have no chance against my skills. Besides, I have to get to my lab. There were a few last minute things I wanted to take care of before I went on my vacation. Maybe I can beat you when I get back."

Jeff gave a wave to her as she stepped to the elevators and said, "Sure thing. I guess I can understand the fear. No, you really shouldn't be ashamed to face me. Really, it is perfectly natural."

Janet gave a coy smile as she pushed the button on the elevator to go to the lab. As the doors closed she yelled, "You fight like a girl!"

Jeff turned back to his game and sighed. *How could a woman so beautiful and smart still be that good at games? Even her taunts during the fights are like songs to me.* He picked up his controller and began another round, however, this one he just didn't have his heart into. It was somewhere else.

Chris made his way to the last key on his trip, the entire set of rounds taking twenty minutes if you walked fast enough. "There, finally finished." Chris said as he placed the last key into the clock to mark his being there. "Now I can go downstairs and get prepared for a few hours of hearty sitting. Sitting, it does the body good."

He triumphantly turned around and began to head toward the staircase leading to the lower floors when he noticed that a door to one of the offices was left open. Chris walked over to close it but was stopped in his tracks by a sudden rustling sound from inside the room.

Damn it, what the hell is this, he said to himself. *Great, someone is in there and I get to go in and find out who it is. What if they have a gun? What am I gonna do? I have a flashlight for crying out loud. The company never wanted to pay for proper gun training, so we get stuck with a damn flashlight. A guy has a gun and I am just supposed to say,* Stop or I'll say stop again! *Meanwhile, I am getting a bullet put into my ass. I need a raise.*

He carefully edged closer to the door trying to remain as silent as possible. Doing his best to imitate every ninja movie he has ever seen, Chris stayed in the shadows as he approached the darkened room, being careful not to make a sound. He contemplated calling down to Jeff at the front desk using the portable radios and telling him to call for help, but he stopped himself realizing that the noise may alert whoever was in the room.

His heart fluttered and his breathing became heavy as he inched closer. Every sound seemed amplified as he tried to remain silent. He was within reach of the door and considered rushing in and yelling to distract the trespasser. Realizing that his meager pay was not worth such a fool hearted effort, Chris resigned himself to simply observe the situation and then decide upon a course of action. As he moved ever closer to the door, he could hear the sounds even more clearly. Chris mustered up enough courage to peer in through the small crack left by the open door, and he let out a gasp of shock at the grotesque sight before him

CHAPTER 2:

SURPRISE

The shock to his system quickly wore off as Chris stared at the sheer horror of the scene taking place in that small office. *How could these things be going on,* was all he could think to himself as he witnessed the bizarre display being played out before him.

"What the hell are you doing? Close the damn door now!" screamed the Senior Vice-President of Maverick Cosmetics, Kyle Levine. It seemed that the good VP was having a little nighttime romp with one of the cleaning ladies. She was a fine woman of only two hundred and fifty pounds with breath that has been known to melt plastic. Really, it was proven.

"I think I will be going now." Chris said as he quickly turned away to not only remove the scene from his sight, but to also hide the losing of his lunch. Ah, pity the poor plant that happened to be next to that doorway.

"Amazing." was all that Alan Salvin could think to say as he sat in the plush seats behind the large viewing window overlooking the laboratory. He stared in sheer astonishment at the sight before him. The room in front of him was a premier example of sterility and efficiency, monitors were carefully placed around the room and cold steel tables lined the center and on them were all manner of animals. However, the one that intrigued him the most was the final table on the right.

Strapped to that table was the guest of honor. A man who was, shall we say borrowed, from the local prison. This was not unusual to see; with all of the overcrowding these days they were only happy to donate a few specimens for the right price. And for what was about to occur, money was no substitute. There were a few failures and some incidents needed to be dealt with, but tonight promised to make the cost and all of his suffering worth it.

"Any time you are ready good doctor." the man urged through the microphone set into the wall.

"Yes sir." was the reply heard through the speakers and then the work was begun. As he readied himself for the task at hand, Dr. Faustus reflected upon the events brought him to this day, the day that would give his life meaning again.

He thought of the strange person that visited him and what was said before he disappeared from his home and into the darkness from where he seemingly appeared.

"I think this is what you were looking for. This is the answer that you seek." the booming voice simply said.

"What is this?" Faustus remarked in astonishment as he studied the strange vial, twisting it in his hands and swirling the strange liquid contained within.

"It is a small sample of what will shed light on your dream." the voice replied, but the doctor was too engrossed in his examination to even notice that he was still in the room, much less speaking to him.

"How did you know about me? Who are you? How do you know what I seek?" were but some of the hundreds of questions going through the revitalized mind of the scientist. *Can I really trust this person?*

"How can you not?" came a response as soon as the question was thought.

The doctor gasped and finally looked at the stranger standing in his home, "How did you know what I was thinking?"

"Simple really, I would be thinking the same thing."

"What do I owe you for this help? Surely there is a price for your assistance. You need something or you would not be here." Faustus said plainly and quickly wished he had not for fear that the opportunity may be taken away as quickly as it was presented. He subconsciously tightened his grip on the vial in fear that it might be taken away from him.

"What I want is not important right now. I will seek you out when the time is right." the mysterious benefactor spoke with a hint of arrogance. "Do you want the gift or not?"

The doctor stood thinking for what felt like ages but was in reality it was only moments. He glanced at his kitchen counter and for the first time in weeks noticed the collection of fungus and insects and decided then that he would no longer live his life in filth. He would know the fruits of his labor. And with a simple word the deal was made.

"Hello, Mr. Salvin." Faustus said as he nervously held the small business card in a shaking hand. He had no idea what to expect when he called the number scrawled on the back. He looked at the remnants of the small vial that lay on his table.

Dr. Faustus began his work at Maverick Cosmetics shortly thereafter. He was given everything he would have needed. Equipment, staffing, funding and most importantly, privacy were all given to him. He was free to conduct his experiments as he saw fit and he wouldn't have wanted it any other way.

His initial experiments were nothing spectacular. He managed to synthesize enough of the Philosopher's Stone to last him for years. That was the first step. The next was the vial. When he first introduced it to the Philosopher's Stone, he was not sure of what to expect. The mixture was added to a cultured sample of the flu virus, the results were remarkable to say the least. Almost instantly the virus was being attacked by the contents of the vial. The sample even remained stable for at least a full minute.

Months of refinement went into the Philosopher's Stone. The amount of each component was measured to the smallest degree. The next few years produced more and more favorable results. The blood samples gradually remained stable for longer periods of time and he had more than a few late night visits from his deep voiced benefactor and the old man. They were both pleased with the reports of his progress and each continued to fulfill his needs as soon as he asked them. Life was good.

Dr. Faustus thought that he had reached Heaven. He had everything he had ever needed: a well stocked lab and the resources to keep it that way. Then came the day that the breakthrough occurred. It was close to daybreak and the doctor was up all night working on the newest batch of the Philosopher's Stone that had been augmented by the liquid from the vial, which was now considered a standard component. He decided to attempt one more experiment before heading to his quarters for some much needed rest. He placed the slide of the flu virus into the microscope. Then he introduced the serum as he had done on many occasions. The usual results occurred, the Philosopher's Stone completely destroyed the virus. The doctor stood back from the microscope, as he had since learned to do, and waited for the explosion. Only none came. One hour went by and nothing happened.

This is it. We are about to pass the threshold. None have lasted longer than an hour, the doctor thought anxiously as he waited for the violent scene to unfold. Two hours, then three passed by with no explosion. *Where's the boom? Where's the lab shattering ka-boom,"* he thought whimsically as he remembered the old cartoons he watched as a child before he discovered science. As the hours ticked by, he finally realized that he had not slept in almost two days. He locked the lab and entered the one code he had waited these many years to use, the code that allowed no one access into the lab until he gave the word.

When he awoke, only a few short hours had passed, but he did not feel the fatigue that would normally accompany him. Only excitement ran through his veins. He quickly raced to the lab to see if his experiment had truly succeeded and he was pleased to note that when he arrived his assistants were busy trying unsuccessfully to gain entry. He peered through the small glass window and noticed that his microscope was still intact. He quickly ran back to his room much to the chagrin of the group of people waiting outside the lab. *Let them wait. I have more important things to do than worry about their feelings,* he thought with glee as he raced back to make the call he had been waiting a lifetime to make.

He burst through his door and went directly to the phone, pausing only to catch his breath and quell the little lights that began to form in front of his eyes. "Hello." he began as the person on the other end of the phone answered. "It is stable." And the other person hung up because no other words were needed.

The lab was cleared; in fact the whole floor was cleared in preparation for the showing. As the time drew nearer to the main event, the doctor became more and more nervous, constantly worried that the sample would erupt at any time and ruin his triumphant day. But it never did. The sample remained stable well after the arrival of Mr. Salvin and the man whom Faustus had later found out was more than just a booming voice in the darkness.

The next few weeks were both exciting and disappointing at best. The first tests on the lab animals showed extremely good progress across all species. All manner of diseases were injected into each creature, from the common cold to HIV. In all cases, the Philosopher's Stone completely wiped out any trace of the illness. The subjects were just as healthy as the day they were born, and for those born with defects, they were better.

Then came the inevitable, human testing. The first round of subjects were "brought in" from the local homeless population with the promise of a meal and a hundred dollars if they only participated. This brought people in by the dozens. While it made for a steady influx of new "material", it also had a side effect. Word of mouths spreads fast among their little community and it wasn't long before there were almost a hundred people that wanted in on the action. That type of attention would simply not do. Secrecy was of the utmost importance at this stage of trials.

The human immune system is an intricate thing and while some of the subjects got well, others had died in the most horrific of ways. Everything from bleeding to death from the inside out to spontaneous combustion occurred over the initial rounds of testing. Over the next few days the amount of homeless people in the city dropped drastically as the doctor was forced to refine his formula for the complexities of the human body. This sudden and mysterious loss of their homeless brethren caused a stir among the population that succeeded in quelling any ideas about participating in the experiments. While this solved the problem of too many wanting to join, it caused the problem of not having enough raw materials.

In need of new subjects, the company went to the most logical place they could think of, the local prisons. It turns out that officials tend to not miss a few prisoners every now and then and with the right amount of compensation, those that were noticed were never reported. As the test subjects remained more and more stable, the amount of inmates needed was lessened. Why pay for new material, when you can simply reuse the ones in storage. Granted it wasn't called storage, the material preferred to call it "housing". Whatever helped them sleep at night was fine with the doctor.

These were not the only sources of material however. At one time, there was a foolish attempt to remove a sample of the cure from the facility to sell to a pharmaceutical company. The person was dealt with most harshly by having been injected with all manner of diseases and cured when they were at their worst only to be injected again and again. Much like Prometheus, who stole fire from the Greek gods and gave it to man, he was doomed to be ruined and revived for as long as time would allow.

Since the attempt, the company was forced to hire a security force assigned to specifically guard the lab. These were not the simply trained guards that patrolled the rest of the building when they were not busy sleeping or goofing off, these specially trained soldiers roamed the halls in equipment purchased directly from various governments around the world. After all, what was the expense of hiring these people compared to the riches to be gained from the cure to end all illness? And to make sure that they all knew what was at stake, as well as to make certain that they were at their best, each soldier was given the option of taking the cure.

While some were reluctant at first, over the weeks of seeing their comrades suffer no side effects caused even the most skeptical to ask for the injection. Some even asked for a family member to be brought in and inoculated. These requests were promptly denied and all personnel were required to sign a non-disclosure agreement upon entering the building. It was easy enough to know if anyone talked since all transmission from the building as well as their homes was monitored. Anyone caught talking or sending an email about the discovery was dealt with, as well as the receiving party.

This brings us back to the glorious night in question. *This is it,* thought Faustus. *I can finally convince the old man to take this public. Once he sees how well it works, he will have no choice but to agree with my findings and make the dream a reality.*

The man strapped to the gurney had been the most un-agreeable of patients. He seemed to think that if he participated, that he would earn his freedom. He would rant to the other subjects about the things he would do on the outside. That was all before he received his first injection of the Ebola virus in preparation of this night. In a matter of a few days the man was sufficiently along with the illness, the original explanation that he was infected with a common flu would no longer stand. Once told of the real illness, the subject was only happy to cooperate and accept the cure, as were those he came in contact with. This provided much in the way of critical data.

The table felt cold, but good against his constantly hot flesh. Blood began to drip from his mouth as he did the only thing his weakened body could do, stare at the ceiling. He couldn't even concentrate enough to think past his own pain. His breaths came in short, steady gasps. He silently prayed that the torment would end and that the cure would work. If not, then Hell had to be better than the pain he was in as he slowly bled to death. Surely Hell had to be better than this.

He never felt the needle penetrate his skin, but he could feel the sudden pain traveling up his arm. He struggled against the tight leather straps, but to no avail. They held his weakened body as firmly as if they were steel. The seconds ticked by like hours as the searing heat in his bloodstream grew to a new crescendo and threatened to drive away what was left of his sanity. He screamed through clenched teeth and after what seemed like an eternity of sheer torment, he simply stopped. Then he began to notice something strange. He could think again.

The pain was there, but it was gradually becoming less intense. The strength that he thought would only wane until he was a withered and bleeding husk on some mad scientist's table began to return. He felt cool, calm and collected for the first time in days. The first thing he noticed was the doctor's grinning face staring at him from above and though he had imagined a multitude of ways to destroy the man, now he felt like kissing that tiny man.

"Feeling better are we?" Faustus asked with a triumphant smile, barely able to contain his excitement. He began to walk around the table making notes on his clipboard. "I trust that you are. You will find that shortly every trace of that or any other illness you may have had will have vanished. But for now I want you to relax. Get dressed and go back to your room. Do not mention the specifics of this to anyone, but tell them that you got better. Tell them that it works."

After the subject finished getting dressed and was being prepared to be escorted back to his room by the security team, the doctor turned to face the observatory window and did his best to suppress the grin that had been on his face since this morning as he said simply, "And there it is gentlemen. You have his file. You know his illnesses. Now, like Lazarus, see him rise. It is finished."

Mr. Salvin simply sat in awe of the experiment, his jaw nearly resting in his lap. Never before had someone been cured at such an advanced state of illness before. He was ready to leave his legacy. Salvin turned to the large man he has learned is called Cheitan and said, "My end of the bargain is complete."

"Indeed." the booming voice echoed from the back of the small room overlooking the laboratory. "Now it is time to finish this arrangement."

A faint glow came from the area around Cheitan. The old man began to weep with the thought of his prize. Those tears quickly became shouts of anger as from the lab a loud crashing could be heard.

Over by the doorway lay the man who moments before was cured, but now laid on the floor in a fetal position screaming of pain and fire, cursing the doctor he so recently praised.

Dr. Faustus slowly began approaching the man as did the four-man security team that rushed in at the sight of what appeared to be a struggle. They stared in stunned silence as the man slowly began to change.

The scream could be heard throughout the entire floor. The cries of anguish were surely heard by all of the floors in the building, as could the crash of the chair upon which Jeff sat only moments before. It seems he didn't share in the pain of his partner at the site of the massive woman being mounted on the desk like a cheap office toy.

The response of, "Hey if you want to get a few pictures of her for your *special notebook*, I am sure there is a camera somewhere on that floor." wasn't quite the sympathetic answer he was looking for. However a chop to the chest had silenced the overwhelming laughter that erupted from Chris' tale of adventure, horror and death. The poor plant, it never saw it coming.

The ringing of the phone brought them both back to their relative senses. Jeff could still be heard laughing even as the phone was removed from the receiver. However, nothing was louder than the annoying voice on the other end.

"I want you two piss-ants down here in my office now!" Captain Corning screamed into the receiver. Before either of them could say anything, he slammed the phone into its cradle and began pacing his office contemplating how he was going to properly punish the fools. When the Vice-President makes a personal visit and demands that someone is fired, it sure as hell wasn't going to be him. He wasn't sure of all of the details, but Corning knew enough to follow orders and get to the bottom of things, but most importantly, he knew how to cover his own ass.

The long walk to the elevator that would take them downstairs was one filled with thoughts of losing the best job they have ever had. Where else can you get paid to play games and sleep? Sure they didn't know they were going to get fired, but there was always that chance when you were called to Corning's office.

The elevator opened into a well-lit hall lined with offices and conference rooms filled with fancy desks and expensive carpeting. The first door to their left was the captain's and he could be heard pacing and breathing heavily even in the hall.

They knocked on the door and heard the captain scream for them to enter. The room smelled like stale pizza and coffee with trash littering the desk. The plush carpet was stained from the many things that had been spilled there. All of that was secondary when compared to the image of the man sitting in the chair opposite Captain Corning. The sight of the vice president made it clear that they were now unemployed.

"It seems that one of you has a problem with entering the offices!" the captain bellowed, his face red with rage. "Mr. Levine tells me that you burst into his office and began shouting at him Chris."

Stunned silence overtook Chris as he stared at the smug face of the man sitting in the simple chair. "But Captain," Chris began to explain once the initial shock had worn off, "I was making…"

"I don't want to hear your excuses!" The irate captain pounded his overly large fist on his desk, knocking over the empty carton of Chinese food and yelled, "I will not stand for your incompetence any longer. You can turn in your uniforms and keys at the end of this shift." Corning sat in his chair, a satisfied look plastered on his round face. You could see the waves of contempt he felt for Chris and Jeff as well as the pure joy that he took in firing them. It was good to be the king.

Chris and Jeff began to protest and explain the situation when suddenly the room went completely dark. It was as if all of the light was simply sucked from the room. The small emergency lights flickered to life, powered by their battery backup, and a small glow was sent throughout the office.

"Now what the hell is going on?" Levine said as he looked at Corning. "Go find out what happened."

"Chris. Jeff. Head to the utility room and check the breakers." Corning ordered.

The duo looked at each other and made their decision. In unison they said, "Bite me." It was worth it to see the shock on the bulbous face of their former boss.

"You just fired us remember?" Jeff said with more than a hint of anger in his voice. It was a side of Jeff that Chris had not often seen and it filled him with pride to see his normally laid back friend stand up to their former tormentor. "You ream us and degrade us every chance you get. You fire us and then you have the audacity to expect us to listen to you? Check it your damn self. We're on a break."

The telltale vein in Corning's forehead was as close to bursting as it had ever been and all in attendance thought he was going to have a stroke on the spot. Instead he just muttered a few obscenities, grabbed his flashlight and stormed off toward the elevator.

Back in the office they could hear him curse as he found out that the elevator wouldn't run without power so the large captain would have to hoof it down a few flights of stairs to reach the generator room. For the first time since they arrived in the office, laughter filled the room. All except the nervous Levine who just sat in his chair trying to make himself disappear all the while wondering what was to become of him now that he was alone with the two men he had just lied about to get fired. The laughter quickly turned to glares of hatred from the two unemployed guards. Chris began to tell the little man just what he thought of him when the room shook and he looked up to see the ceiling crashing down around him. He brought his hands up to protect himself as best he could. Then the world went dark.

CHAPTER 3:

THE LONG WALK

The scene in the lab was one of utter chaos. Lab equipment was strewn about in such disarray that it was hard to tell where it all belonged. Beakers containing various liquids no longer sat in their neat little shelves; monitors lie shattered upon the cold tile floor and the pristine steel lab tables were overturned. However, this was nothing compared to the scene unfolding.

The man who had most recently been cured was now a heap on the floor screaming and writhing in agony. The terrible sound that came from the strained throat gurgled as if the air could not escape his lungs. The man was drowning on his own blood.

What could have happened, Faustus thought worriedly as he saw his life's ambition slowly slip away with each garbled scream of the subject lying on the floor. *Everything was going so well. It held in others.*

In the lab's observation room, the now frantic Salvin stared in shock at the sight before him. Alan Salvin had seen many things in his life but this indeed was a horrific sight to behold. His life's work was being destroyed. The large figure next to him simply stood there. Even among the chaos of the destruction, he was as strong and stoic as ever. "Security." Cheitan announced through the lab's intercom. "Take that man back to the holding cells and then report to the security room. I want a full report on the condition of the building on Mr. Salvin's desk in ten minutes."

"We need to go to your office now Mr. Salvin." Cheitan said in a way that Salvin was sure it was more an order than a request.

Salvin's office was a short trip down the hallway. Passing scared and confused employees without even giving them a glance, much less an explanation; they entered the large room and closed the reinforced double doors behind them. The lock clicked into place as they moved toward the large desk situated in the back of the room. This wasn't his main office, but having one this close to the labs had proved more than convenient on many occasions.

However, the once neat and orderly office was thrown into a whirlwind of torment. Volumes of text that, at one time lined the neatly kept shelves, littered the floor and threatened to destroy the precious works. Priceless art was scattered on the floor among the common trash, shredded and torn beyond repair. The timeless pieces now were worth less than the scraps of paper that accompanied them. In the far corner, where a Ming vase was once proudly displayed in a glass case, was where the remains of the same vase laid shattered beyond all recognition on the hardwood floor below.

Still all of these things were nothing compared to what he lost this night.

"What the hell happened?" Salvin gasped as he attempted to regain his breath with the oxygen mask he placed over his age-lined face. It seems that age was quickly catching up with him and youth was the one thing that all of his wealth could not buy. He built an empire making people appear younger, but true youth was never to be his again.

"This was an unexpected outcome. We need to make sure that this does not get out," Cheitan calmly stated as he gestured toward the emergency lockdown panel that would not only make sure that no one left the building, but also that none were permitted entry. The series of switches and commands that would cause the entire building to be sealed in case of just such an occasion were located in the most obvious of places, the large desk behind which Salvin sat with utter fear etched across his weathered features. This was one of Mr. Salvin's brighter ideas, and Cheitan was more than willing to let him think that he came up with it. Now to get the generators started.

Corning awoke to find himself in the stairwell. Debris was scattered everywhere. Plaster from the wall and ceiling littered the passage. He could smell the faint hint of smoke rising from below. If the power wasn't restored quickly and the sprinkler system activated, the entire building could become one giant fireball. That was the problem with storing thousands of gallons of chemicals in the building you work in.

The dust choked his lungs as he navigated the mostly intact flight of stairs all the while thanking God that his flashlight wasn't damaged. The going was slow thanks the general condition of his surroundings, but he was determined to finish his assignment. "Without me, this whole place will crumble. What will they do when I retire? At least those two simpletons won't be around to screw things up." Corning said to no one in particular.

The trip to basement level three was uneventful if not slow going thanks to the scattered pieces of the office building lying everywhere and caused him to fill the empty area with the most colorful of curses as he stumbled and tripped over one piece of rubble after another.

The room seemed as though someone had filled it with liquid shadow. Nothing could be seen anywhere. The slight groans coming from the darkness served as the only means of locating someone.

"What in the Hell was that?" Jeff exclaimed as he slowly came to his senses. Shoving the room off of himself, he stood to only to smash his head on a hanging fluorescent light fixture. After that new pain had somewhat subsided and joined the rest of the new aches in his body, Jeff choked out a call to his compatriot. "Are you alive, Chris?"

"I'm ok." came a reply from a weakened voice somewhere off in the corner of the now decimated office.

"I didn't ask you." Jeff growled as he searched for his fallen comrade all the while swearing that if Chris died and that prick lived, he would make sure that he never made it out of the room. "Levine, it's your damn fault we're in here! If you wouldn't have to polish your desk with Mrs. Clean, then we wouldn't have been down here to be knocked unconscious right now. And I swear if anything happened to Chris, I will kill you."

If light were to permeate the room even for a fraction of a second, Jeff would see that the once proud executive had created a small puddle beneath himself.

Suddenly a voice screamed from the darkened room, "Will you both shut the fuck up! I just had a damn room fall on my head! Son of a bitch, I need an aspirin."

Jeff would never show it, but relief began to show in his eyes as he heard the condescending voice of his partner. Even when he complained the most, even when his mood would be at its most sour, Jeff always stood by his friend.

"Hey," Jeff began, "I am glad you are alive and all, but I really wanted your PS2."

"Even if I was battered and lying in a pool of my own fluids, which I think I am, you would never get my PS2." Chris replied with a grin as he climbed from under the fallen ceiling tiles and pieces of plaster.

The sigh coming from Levine could only be described as one of pure relief. He knew his chances of surviving this predicament were slim, but now with both of the guards to protect him and guide him out, he should be fine. Now, his only problem was how to get them to take him to the main entrance.

The large metal door inscribed with the large, white letters B3 signified he had reached his destination. He pushed the latch and entered the silent room filled with large machines normally humming with a life of their own. The eerie silence filled the room and seemed to amplify every step he made, not that his girth made the going any lighter.

Suddenly the generators kicked on seemingly of their own accord. "Huh," Corning began to complain, "I made this damn trip for nothing. Almost got crushed, hurt my ankle and had to run down two freaking flights of stairs! I am really going to kill those two. I'm just glad my asthma went away. I really need to thank that doctor. He is a bit of a freak though."

Turning to leave the room, Corning prepared himself for the trip upstairs and swore that when he got to his office, there would be Hell to pay. No one disobeys his orders. No one.

A large shadow stepped out from behind a generator and watched as Corning left. He made his way back to Salvin's office to begin the lockdown process.

Dr. Faustus sat in his office surrounded by volumes of experiments and research notes pouring over each one with the attention only the mad could provide. He was thankful that the lights were back on and he didn't need to use his tiny book light to read with any longer. The trip through the holding area was one met with questions and shouts of anger and confusion, but Faustus had no time for the petty concerns of the subjects and rushed by them to the safety of his office.

"How could this happen." Faustus nervously asked himself while at the same time trying to ward off a breakdown. It would do no good to lose it now. "The other subjects in the holding area were fine. They seemed to show no ill side effects. What was so different about this one?" Delving into the man's personal and medical history, Faustus was determined to make sure that this mistake was not his own and that it would never happen again.

The subject was perfectly healthy before he arrived here. He was given nothing that would react violently with the serum. Did we let his disease progress too far along? These and a myriad of other questions raced through the frantic mind of the doctor as he attempted in vain to isolate that one lost variable that had destroyed his day, his dream. He had to have another look at the body.

"And I want you to take me back upstairs and let me out of this building." Levine said plainly while attempting to sound like he retained some of his former authority.

The laughter that erupted from the two former security guards filled the entire hall and caused tears to well up into their eyes.

"Let me get this straight," Chris began between fits and gasps of breath, "you expect us to take you to the outside? Let me think about that. Um, no. You screw us over and then have the nerve to think you can tell us what to do? Not bloody likely." Turning to his hysterical partner, Chris said, "Come on Jeff, I think there is a cafeteria on this floor. Let's get us a few snacks."

"Dude, we have no cash." Jeff protested as he finished dusting the rest of the debris off of himself.

"Maybe not, but I think a free meal is the least this company can do for us after dropping a building on our heads. Besides, the machines may be broken anyway; we will just be saving the food. It hates to go to waste you know." Chris finished with a grin and then began to leave the room when the most unexpected thing happened.

Jeff felt something attempting to hold him in the room. He turned and glared at the sheer testicular fortitude of the tiny executive. Imagine him grabbing Jeff by the arm and attempting to keep him there while saying that the duo had to take him topside. That is was their job.

The fist to the face was not what Levine expected and as he crumpled to the floor, he realized that he really should have thought through his plan a little more.

The holding area was one of confusion and anger. The *guests* were becoming more and more restless and many wished that they had stayed in prison. Questions echoed through the long halls and the fear was so evident you could almost smell it. Some of the prisoners wondered when they could go home, while others worried about their missed meal and still others were concerned if anyone would come for them at all. After all, who would look through the rubble for them who were the forgotten of society? They were only inmates after all.

Even when the lights returned they could not help but wonder what their fate would be. Especially after seeing the shape of the last person brought in.

Mr. Salvin breathed a little easier when he noticed the lights return. However, he could not feel truly safe until he saw Cheitan enter through the double doors and signal for the lockdown to commence.

The series of commands were given, the password entered and the appropriate switches were flipped and at their completion, the entire building was sealed shut. Steel plates shuttered themselves over the windows and doorways, guaranteeing that none would leave or enter this place. It was time.

Chris and Jeff entered the cafeteria and marveled at the site before them. Sure there was, what became the usual, pieces of the building scattered everywhere, but what really amazed the duo was the sheer amount of food.

"Dear God man!" Chris exclaimed wide-eyed with shock. "Can you believe this? Why have we never been down here before? They have fifteen vending machines! And they are all stocked fresh! The most we had was that overcharging monstrosity that had only the most rock-hard stale candy from the Seventies."

Jeff's only response was, "Look, over at that last machine. They have Chinese food! I think this is Heaven." Then they casually strolled up to their first victim and began to delve into its contents, devouring everything in sight as though it were their last meal. In their defense, they did this at every meal. There was a literal smorgasbord of choices. Everything from hot meals to soft drinks and candy were theirs for the taking.

After an hour of self-indulgence, they rested casually on the tables that were still upright. "So now what?" Jeff moaned as he tried to fight off the effects of an overstuffed stomach.

Chris replied, equally in pain, "First, I think the whole building falling on us hurt less than this and secondly, I think we should get the Hell out of here."

Levine waited for about twenty minutes before he got the courage to pull himself from the floor. In that time he managed to convince himself that it was a lucky shot and a lowly guard could never truly best him. *How dare he lay his hands on me?* Levine thought to himself. *Once I get to the surface, my lawyers will have a field day ruining his life and taking whatever meager possessions he holds dear.*

Realizing that he would have to get himself out of this situation, he began to take a walk to the stairwell. Halfway down the hall he peered through the large glass windows into the cafeteria and marveled at the scene of pure gluttony before him. *How can they even look at themselves? Peasants lining up to the feeding trough like pigs. I will make them pay.*

He continued the rest of the way down the hall to the stairs and was startled as he opened the door, he ran headlong into Captain Corning. *Good, maybe this simpleton can be coaxed to take me upstairs.*

Corning made his trip up the long stairwell with even less grace then he descended it. Maybe he should have spent more time exercising and less time on his ass. When he reached for the door-handle that would take him to the hallway to his office, he was almost run into by the pompous little man Levine. *Man I hate these uppity types. Then again, he did help me get rid of the two morons, so he can't be all bad. Still, tossing him down these flights of stairs might be fun.*

After a few brief minutes and a greatly exaggerated tale of what happened since he left, Corning agreed that he should do two things. First, he would lead the whiner upstairs. Then he would come back and deal with the losers. A stern beating was indeed in order.

Even before they reached the first set of stairs of their trip, Corning was once again ready to toss the tiny man down the staircase. If he had to hear one more time of how he was mistreated, Corning would show him real mistreatment.

"…and then the bastard hits me! ME! Can you believe the sheer audacity?" Levine complained again, but the rest of the ranting had taken a back seat to what could only be described as pure, unadulterated Hell.

The pain in the pit of Corning's stomach felt like tiny shards of glass tearing through his midsection with a razor's precision and a mad surgeon's will. It felt like thousands of scalpels making skin-deep incisions so that the patient lived and still felt every cut. Every slice was a piece of torment in itself and felt as though it was amplified by the pouring of salt into the wound. The pain was not only located in his middle, it spread throughout his entire body until the only thing that he felt was the stinging pain that was sure to drive him mad if it did not kill him first. His hands, arms and other extremities were alight with the same feeling as he tore at his clothing to try to remove whatever was causing this. His brain was fire in its most primal form. It seared with one thought, to stop the pain.

Dr. Faustus decided that more tests were in order. *Yes, more tests. Once I do more tests, I can find out where the extraneous variable entered. It may be any of a thousand possibilities. Hopefully the others are not suffering the same fate as the other subject. Their continued progress must signify that the problem was with the subject and not my cure.* So, with his new goal in mind, he set off toward the holding area.

The holding area was a mass of chaos; the doors to most of the cells were shattered into splinters. The confused subjects wandered around aimlessly busy trying to determine exactly what happened. One of them noticed the doctor turn the corner and began to quickly approach him. Some would even say that they were stalking towards him like predators sensing a wounded animal. Instantly the others fell in behind all shouting questions ranging from what happened to when were they going to be released.

Dr. Faustus calmly told them everything they wanted to hear in order to keep them from getting out of control and overtaking the little man.

"What happened to Mike?" one of them asked obviously more concerned with his own well-being.

"He had an accident." Faustus replied in an attempt to not only conceal the truth, but to also make sure they did not rend him limb from limb. "However, steps are being taken to make sure that this type of thing does not happen again. I want all of you to come to the lab so that I can run a few tests to determine exactly what happened. Follow me."

Reluctantly the crowd followed him to the lab all the while unsure of whether or not they would actually make it back.

As they approached the lab, they were murmuring nervously among themselves. However, all eyes quickly turned to see what had caused the excruciating scream from behind them. It was Alex. He was doubled over in pain and his face was a mask of terror. He gazed up at his fellow prisoners and looked into their eyes pleading for someone to help him or put him out of his misery. Blood red tears flowed from the once proud man and even the most hardened among them could not help but pity the poor soul.

The doctor ignored all this as he began to open the door of the laboratory. His entire being was focused on one goal, completing his cure. After all, what were the concerns of mere lab rats with one who was going to save the world?

When will they stop complaining and realize their rightful place? It is truly an honor to be one of the harbingers of peace and these peasants complain as if it is a burden, Faustus thought to himself as he slid his card through the electronic lock and entered the only password that would open the laboratory door. Suddenly from behind him it wasn't just the mild complaints of one of the subjects, it was a chorus of terror filled screams that sounded as though they came from the darkest pits of Hell.

When Faustus turned to see what the commotion was all about, his eyes went wide with horror. All of the men he brought with him were writhing around the floor in pools of their own blood. All rational thought had left him. For that moment he was not the brilliant scientist who would one day bring hope to the world, his only desire was to get away from that screaming.

He rushed into the lab and slammed the door behind him quickly engaging electronic lock and entering the code would allow no others entry. As his safety became apparent, protected as he was by thick steel walls and bulletproof glass, he could once again become the dedicated scientist. He peered through the glass at this grotesque scene unfolding before him, carefully analyzing the situation and assessing possible outcomes and causes.

The subjects had begun tearing and clawing and each other in an attempt to remove themselves from the gore soaked floor. Slowly they began to right themselves and the doctor could hear the pleading questions from those that could still speak. They screamed for him to help them. Blood smeared hands streaked the window and the fear-etched faces begged for death.

Mr. Salvin sat behind his desk staring at the bank of monitors that showed him images from every part of his building. His face was locked in a permanent state of shock. He glanced over his shoulder and noticed that for the first time ever Cheitan smiled.

The man stood before Salvin, looked down at him and said, "Our bargain is complete. It is done."

Chapter 4:

The Gathering

The bloated masses rose up and slowly walked towards the doors, shuffling their feet as they went. Soft groaning could be heard throughout the entire floor. The pain they felt emanated from them in waves.

"Dude, I think those burritos were bad." Jeff moaned as he reached for the handle to the cafeteria door. "Maybe they weren't green chili. They tasted OK though."

Straining to remain upright Chris clutched at his abdomen in hopes that it would not spill its contents all over the once neatly polished floor. "Let's just be thankful for the free meal and get out of this death trap. I don't need another section of this building falling on me. My head hurts enough. It does feel pretty good to know that the chubby prick Corning will be waddling up and down the stairs cursing our names the whole time. Maybe we'll get lucky and he'll have a heart attack. We can't be fired if he's dead."

"I'll just be happy if we live through this." Jeff replied. He stopped suddenly and stood with an expression of fear and concern etched upon his face. "SHIT!"

At the sudden exclamation Chris straightened up, at great discomfort to his personal being, and checked the surroundings for any sign of something wrong. Not that he would be leaping into action any time soon; he just wanted to know when to get the hell out of the way. "What are you screaming about?"

"In all this confusion, I forgot to check on my game." Jeff answered with a worried tone.

"And my system and TV!" Chris replied with equal shock and terror in his voice. "Get your ass moving! We need to get upstairs now!"

And with that they were off at a slight jog, the pain in their stomachs allowed little else. Jeff grabbed a mop that one of the janitorial staff had left behind, Chris was sorry he hadn't thought to pick up the makeshift walking stick to aid him along in the long trek to the now working elevator.

They arrived at the first floor, ever thankful that the elevator still worked and they didn't take a long drop to their untimely deaths. However, this good feeling was quickly replaced by one of dread as they noticed their mangled workstation. The wailing of the damned would not equal the pain felt as Jeff noticed the shattered remnants of his new game. Chris silently mourned for the loss of his game system and television. A soft, somber voice could be heard to say, "Rest in Peace".

After giving him a few minutes to collect himself, Chris slowly helped Jeff to his feet. They walked to the front door with tears in their eyes. As they reached for the handle it was then that they realized something was wrong, aside from the whole building collapsing on them thing. It wasn't that the doors were locked, which would have been no real surprise as they locked the doors themselves. It was the large metal shutters that shocked them mostly.

More than a bit curious, they decided to see if they could get out any other way. They continued to check all of the other sections of the first floor, but all of the side doors and windows were covered with these steel plates.

"What in the hell is going on here?" Jeff asked with more than a bit of concern evident in his voice. All the pain from their meal and the loss of a precious loved one was gone when they realized just what they were...trapped.

"Jeff, I think we died in that elevator and this is Hell. Doomed to forever patrol these halls and not be able to have a game system." Chris said in his best horror movie voice. "We have gone to Security Guard Hell."

"Well great," Jeff replied throwing his hands in the air in frustration, "now I have to spend eternity with you re-telling your old stories again and again. Like I haven't heard each one a hundred thousand times. Now it will be a million years of 'Dude, do you remember when'. Wake me up next millennia."

"Can't sleep man. The chairs got busted when the ceiling fell." Chris told his partner.

"NO!" Jeff's scream echoed into the hollow lobby as he noticed the wrecked chairs lying on the floor. "Why do you hate me God?"

Over the sound of Jeff sobbing Chris said, "Let's go find Corning and see if he can't let us out of here. He has to know a way to raise these gates." And with that simple goal in mind they headed to the stairwell, not willing to press their luck with the elevator another time.

Jeff grabbed at the door handle and as he opened it, he saw that the stairway was littered with shattered pieces of building and realized that these things would make the going slow. He was glad for his precious walking stick. As they started down the stairs, lit only by the few hanging fluorescent lights that remained intact, Chris called down to Jeff, "Dude, it is not that bad. You can stop with the grumbling and complaining."

Confused, Jeff looked back at his friend and answered, "It wasn't me man. I was just about to call you a wussy."

Both of them searched for direction of the noise, but with the vast echo in the stairway, it was difficult to pinpoint exactly where the sound was coming from. Deciding that even though it was no longer their job to give a damn, they continued to navigate the debris down towards the entrance to the office level where the sound appeared to be coming from.

Professor Faustus had long since learned to keep himself detached from his subjects. To think of them as anything other than the materials they were would cause a person to care about them, and that could hinder your objectivity and cause your results to be compromised. Still, even he felt a small amount of pity for the grisly sight displayed before him. The screaming had finally stopped and the men were just lying there on the floor. Once their screams had subsided, Faustus considered stepping outside of his safe haven in order to check on the subjects. This caused another thought to occur to him, where was the security team? Surely they had heard the screams.

He reached for the handset next to the doorway and dialed the extension for the head of security, not that bloated Corning and his team of incompetents; he was looking for the real security for the building. An answer never came and Faustus replaced the receiver and reached for the keypad to open the door. As he opened the door carefully in case one of the surely angry subjects attempted to rush him, he heard the groaning sounds of people in pain.

Good, some of them are still alive, he thought to himself, anxious to get back to his experiments and eager to discover what had gone so terribly wrong. The doctor gasped in shock at the sight before him. With as much speed as he could muster, he slammed the door shut and vowed to never leave the sanctuary of his lab. He slid down against the door to not only hide himself, but to hide the gruesome scene from his eyes. Never had he seen such a display of wanton carnage. *That is not true now is it?* He thought to himself, his rational mind attempting to reassert itself over the sheer terror that had since replaced any real thought. *You have seen this before. Sure it was only in the movies, but you know what this is, don't you?*

Why won't that little piss-ant shut his hole? Corning struggled to retain any kind of rational thought as he tried to hold onto consciousness. Slowly he felt himself slipping into the blinding pain, it was overwhelming him. The only sounds that now escaped from his dry throat were gasps and moans, when what he truly wanted to do was scream. He couldn't figure out what had happened to cause this. Why was he being punished?

Corning lowered himself none to gently to the stairs much to the protesting of Levine. *Maybe if I just close my eyes and rest a moment, this will pass. Then I can pay a visit to the good doctor downstairs.* These were the last thoughts that Captain Corning had as he slipped into that final sleep.

"What are you doing you fat, lazy, imbecile?" Levine shouted down at the prone man once he noticed Corning slump down onto the stairs. He went and began to shake the still form of Corning all the while shouting at him to follow him and unlock the front door. That was when he heard the sounds of footsteps and voices coming from overhead.

"Hey, what happened to Blimpy?" Jeff asked as he rounded the stairwell and saw the large from of Corning lying on the stairs and Levine slapping him in the face.

"Can you believe he fell asleep?" Levine complained. "He is supposed to be escorting me upstairs and the lazy bastard falls asleep."

Chris rounded the corner and took in the scene, "Just out of curiosity, you are not expecting us to give a damn or anything about the two of you are you? The only reason we are not on our way home is because of the steel shutters all over the doors and windows. We figured Sleeping Ugly there might have a way to open them."

Staring in disbelief, Levine looked at the two former guards and said, "So what you are telling me is that we are locked in here? No way out? Right. Like a cosmetics company is going to have that kind of security. Give me a break."

A look of sheer delight came over the face of Levine as he said, "I know why you two are really down here. You want to beg for your jobs back don't you? Well, let me tell you that there is…" The last of that sentence was cut short as the only sounds in the narrow stairwell were the sharp intake of breath from the two guards, the pain filled scream from Levine, and the loud tearing of flesh from Levine's arm.

"Holy Shit!" That was the scream that came in unison from the two former guards as they watched the scene unfold before them. Were they really seeing their former boss eating the man that got them fired? The blood soaked face of the thing that was once Corning looked up at them and they then realized that they were not moving. That was enough to get them to launch themselves up the stairs that they just spent all of that time climbing down.

The door to the first floor was quickly opened and slammed shut as they leaned against it and panted for the better part of a minute before the shock began to wear off and they were able to speak.

"Chris, what the fuck was that?" Jeff asked in a panic stricken voice.

"Dude, how many times have we seen just what the fuck that was? How many games, movies and books was that in?" Chris said staring into the lobby before him just praying that nothing else was in there with them.

"If you tell me that the Captain was just turned into what I think you are going to tell me, I am going to kick you in the nuts." Jeff stated in a matter of fact tone.

"But it is just that, the Cap is a…" The phrase was cut short by the sound of something pounding on the other side of the door. Sliding and scraping noises were joined by moans of torment and hunger.

Alan Salvin sat in his high backed leather office chair and stared at the being before him. He has never deluded himself. He knew that he had made a pact with the devil, but this particular devil didn't want his immortal soul, it just wanted his help and for what was being offered in return, help was the least he could do.

As he stared in a shard of broken mirror at the youthful and handsome face he remembered from those many years ago, he could not help but think that this was his second chance to make his mark, to leave his true legacy.

"We are finished here Mr. Salvin." Cheitan said as he completed the man's transformation from weakened old man to the youthful appearance he now displayed. Cheitan then strode from the room to find another with which he made a bargain. *It is time for my dream to become a reality. Soon I will show them all what it means to defy me, and then Hell itself will tremble at my name.*

Dr. Faustus paced back and forth in his lab unable to drown out the moans of the *Go ahead and say it, zombies. You created zombies.* Frantically searching for some answer as to why this happened and what could be done about it, Faustus tore into his research notes with the voracity of a cornered wolverine fully comforted by the knowledge that no one was able to get into his reinforced lab.

"Hello Doctor"

Faustus screamed at the sound of the voice and threw his precious notes unceremoniously into the air where they proceeded to scatter across the lab among the spilled chemicals and other agents.

"How did you get in here?" Faustus asked through panting breaths as he struggled to calm his heart into something resembling a normal rhythm.

"Really Marlin, after all this time, you need to ask me things like that?" Cheitan said with a hint of laughter. "I just stopped by to tell you that our arrangement is complete. Thank you for your help, but you are no longer needed."

"What are you talking about? You have not completed your end of the deal!" Faustus said almost livid with rage and fear. "My cure is not finished. Just look around you!" Faustus exclaimed, gesturing at the throng of bloody beings pounding uselessly at the bulletproof glass of the lab.

A straightforward smile spread over the face of Cheitan as he stated in a calm tone, "Simple really. You wanted the pathetic beings of this world free from the trappings of disease and now they will be."

Taken aback at the dismissive tone of the creature before him, Faustus screamed, "Look at them! You call them cured?"

"No Doctor. I do not. However, they never have to worry about disease again, as was our bargain."

"Then how can you possibly claim to have held up your end of our deal?" Faustus pleaded. "I should have known better than to trust the likes of you." Faustus glared at Cheitan with such anger and hatred that belied the little man's size.

"How dare you speak to me in such a tone! Were it not more amusing to watch you suffer for the rest of your pathetic and short life, I would kill you here and now." Without another word Cheitan turned towards a shadowed corner of the lab. Faustus was behind him firing all manner of questions and accusations at him. Cheitan stopped and turned to face Dr. Faustus. "On second thought…" Cheitan said as he glanced at the tiny man before him. Reaching out with one of his powerful arms, he grabbed Dr. Faustus around the throat and lifted him off of the floor.

"You see good doctor," Cheitan began and he stared into the bulging eyes of the little insect he held in an iron-like grip, "you have just outlived your usefulness. In case you were EVER having delusions of you being anything more than a tiny piece of my plan, this should put your role into perspective."

Cheitan leaned forward until he was eye to eye with the doctor who was turning a shade of blue reserved for those on the brink of death. With a sudden jerk of his wrist and a loud snapping like dozens of chicken bones being crushed under the boot of a giant, the doctor's face went slack and the life left his eyes. He was dropped to lie among the debris-strewn floor like so much garbage. Without even a glance back, Cheitan melted into the shadows.

Cheitan left Faustus lying in the filth that so represented his life and retired to a room he had secured for himself. He began to think of this room as his sanctuary, a place to contemplate his plans and his future. Now, however, it was a place to rest. He needed to gather his strength for the coming conflicts that he knew were inevitable. His plans would not go unnoticed for long and then the true tests would begin.

"How long can this possibly go on?" Chris said tiredly as they stood in the same place they had been for fifteen minutes still hearing the scraping and groaning of their former boss. "Wasn't it enough that he tormented us when he was alive, now that he is a zombie he has to keep it up!"

"I thought I told you not to use that word!" Jeff yelled over the constant barrage of noise from the other side of the door. "Okay, we need to get out of here. Captain Corpse in there may have known a way out, but alas, he will not be much help."

"Right," Chris agreed, "but we still need to get our asses out of here. That is the main plan at this point."

A look of shock and sudden realization came over the face of Jeff. "Oh crap." he simply said in a tone almost unheard over the relentless pounding on the other side of the door.

"What?"

"Janet."

"Oh, you have got to be kidding me." Chris said looking at his long time friend and praying that he didn't mean what he thought he meant. "You can't possibly want to go back down there. Do you know how many of them there are?"

"So far just the one," Jeff said simply and pleading with his friend.

"There is ALWAYS just the one! Then you get into the deep dark places and BANG; there are a million of them! Hell no. Besides, how can you be sure that she isn't already one of them?" Chris babbled in a tone that meant he was going to hold fast in his convictions.

"Well, " Jeff began, "I don't know how many there are and I am not sure if she is one or not, but would you want me to come looking for you if you were down there?"

"Fucking guilt trips. Fine, but if I get eaten, I am so kicking your ass. Now, first we deal with the guy trying to eat us." Chris said unable to find fault in his friend for wanting to save someone he felt was important.

Relief showed on Jeff's face as the two began to plan how to best get out of their current situation.

"Well, this certainly is interesting." She sat on one of the few chairs left undamaged in the lounge that was reserved for lab techs and pondered on just what had happened. One minute she was standing outside the lab of Dr. Faustus, waiting to see what was going on inside that lab, and the next Dr. Faustus told the group of onlookers to hang around in here until his experiment was completed. That was before the building shook.

Now she sat there among the other rejected scientists that were not important enough to see what was so significant that Faustus made them all leave his precious area.

"Well." She said to no one in particular. "I guess I might as well get out of here before the rest of this place decides to pay me a visit. Now, where was that stairway again?"

Janet stepped out of the room and glanced at the destruction before her. After seeing the state of the area around her, she could only imagine the turmoil that her work area was in.

I may have to cancel that vacation. The place is a wreck. She thought about how she was going to have to replace most of her samples and that would probably put her over her budget for the next year at least.

Taking a right out of the waiting area, Janet walked down the hall towards her lab. As she neared the main hallway, she heard something she never thought she would ever hear outside of her nightmares. She paused before reaching that crucial intersection and flattened herself up against the wall.

The wailing of the group of people that was coming from the direction of Dr. Faustus lab was maddening to say the least. *Lucky for me, they haven't seen me yet.*

As she turned and started to go back to the relative safety of her little waiting area, she ran headlong into an overturned potted plant which caused her to go crashing to the floor. A small yelp of pain escaped her lips. That was quickly followed by a curse of her own luck as she realized that the moaning of whatever those things were was getting louder. That could only mean one thing. They were getting closer.

CHAPTER 5:

LOST AND FOUND

Chris and Jeff stood with their backs pressed against the steel doorway. They knew what needed to be done and they knew they had to get it done quickly if they were ever going to be able to save not only Janet, but themselves as well. The pounding and moaning that came from the other side seemed to increase as time went on. It was as though the creature knew that food was near and was becoming more and more determined to reach its prize.

"OK." Chris said as the kept the pressure on the door. "First thing we need is a weapon. We already know enough about these things to know how to kill them. Now all we need is a shotgun, a magnum pistol and a rocket launcher."

"Maybe a set of lock picks too," Jeff added with a forced smile.

"Exactly, now since we have none of those and no access to any of those things, I would say we are officially screwed. We need to look around here and find something so that we can do this quickly. The less chance he has to eat us, the happier I am." As the door rocked from a seemingly endless barrage from their former boss, Chris couldn't help but think that he really wished he had called in sick today.

The two former guards began glancing around the destroyed lobby for signs of anything that could be used as a weapon. Ceiling tiles and plants littered the place. Doors to offices were lying on the floor. That was when inspiration struck.

"Hey Chris." Jeff began hoping that he had found a solution that would finally end this standoff. "What about one of those large paper cutters? You know the ones with the machete attached to them? There was one in that office on the second floor. Third one on the left, I think." Jeff was beaming at the thought of having found a suitable weapon.

"How do you know there's one in there? When have you ever needed one of those? You don't believe in paperwork." Chris asked skeptically.

"I use it all the time for cutting the crust off of my sandwiches."

"OK, now which one of us will go and get this thing? Because you know that the one that doesn't has to hold this door closed right?" Chris asked.

"I guess it comes down to Rock, Paper, Scissors again, doesn't it? Loser stays."

"No." Chris sighed, resigning himself to his new position as doorstop. "As little as I relish the thought of holding the door and keeping Captain Cadaver from munching on my succulent brains, you know where this thing is. You can get it faster. Just make damn sure you run."

Jeff nodded and headed towards the short flight of stairs that lead to the second floor offices.

"Sure am glad it took so much to convince you to just leave me here to die!" Chris shouted at the retreating form of his partner.

Janet picked herself up off of the floor and without even a quick glance to see how close those things were behind her; she took off as fast as she could to the relative safety of the waiting area she just left.

As she closed the door she managed to catch a glimpse of the image of sheer terror that was shambling down the hallway towards her one time sanctuary. She knew she could not stay there, but she also realized that she could not abandon those others that were in the room with her.

They don't know. She thought. *They are lying here on the floor of this building that could kill them at any moment and they have no idea that a worse thing is coming for them just outside this flimsy door.*

She stood staring at her fallen co-workers and resolved herself to getting them roused and forming some type of plan to escape. Realizing that leaving through the door was not an option, she began to think of other methods and she went to each of the five scientists and attempted to rouse them from their seemingly endless and sound sleep.

"Come on guys." She said to their prone forms all the while keeping a close watch one the door. "We have to get out of here now."

Fear rising in her as she was not only failing to wake her colleagues, but also because she could plainly hear the first footfalls arriving outside the door, Janet decided that she needed to take drastic actions. She tried everything from slapping them awake to pouring cold and hot water on them. Nothing was working. Then she heard one of them begin to stir. The sound was coming from the far corner and while there was not very much light in the decimated room, she could see that the person was trapped under a fallen fluorescent light.

Janet quickly raced over to the man and began to help him out of the wreckage when she heard another soft moan from behind her. Her first thoughts were that the things had gotten through the door, but Janet realized that she would have heard them enter. *What could be making that sound then?* She thought to herself.

Before Janet could turn to see what was going on a strong hand gripped her forearm and a wail erupted from in front of her. The very man she had just been trying to help had a hold of her and was attempting to...

That's just not possible! Her rational mind tried to tell itself even as the first hand created a hole in the door of her safe room. She wrenched her arm free from the man on the floor and stood to look for an exit. She came nearly face to face with something that, at one time, was a woman she had almost been friends with. Now this person was barely recognizable, as blood had begun to pour from her eyes to stream over her chin and land in an ever-growing puddle on the floor.

Staring into the foggy eyes of her assistant she had time to think, *How will I get out of here?*

Alan Salvin finally pulled himself away from the mirror he had been gazing into. He began busying himself with the clean up of his office. After he replaced the items that were not shattered beyond repair, he took in the rest of his collection that could never be replaced. "So many beautiful things were destroyed. So many things that can never be taken back." He could not hold back his disgust with himself for the small amount of joy that his newfound youth had brought him. He felt ashamed as he took a final look in the mirror before returning to his desk.

Mr. Salvin made no delusions about what he was a part of. He knew what Cheitan was from the first moment he appeared in his office, but at that time, he had been an old man. A man who knew that his time with this world was drawing nearer. As Salvin stared into the monitors lining the walls, he saw scenes unfolding all around the building. He noted the prisoner paddock was trashed and empty, which meant that they were wandering around the floor that his office was located upon. He saw that his highly paid security team was no longer patrolling the floors of his building. He glanced over the rest of the monitors before he settled himself into his large chair and began to wonder just how long he was going to be trapped in here before he was finally released.

Alan reached for a button to a private intercom that connected himself to Cheitan's private quarters. "Cheitan. Are you there?"

Cheitan sat on the cold floor of his sanctuary silently gathering his strength for the conflict that was sure to happen when he was interrupted by the whining little human. "What is it you want now, Mr. Salvin?" Cheitan replied not bothering to hide the irritation he felt at the disturbance.

"How long do you plan on having the building locked down?" Alan continued.

Frustrated, Cheitan suppressed the chiding comments he had building and said, "I need a few more hours for the effects to become permanent. Once that is done, you will be free to go wherever you wish." *If the fool knew the real reason he could not open those shutters, surely he would end his miserably short existence now. Maybe I should tell him just to watch the look on his face.*

Cheitan contemplated this as he broke the connection to Mr. Salvin and resumed his meditation. *He will know soon enough.*

Chris heard Jeff coming down the stairs, hopefully with the prize in hand. Jeff caught sight of his friend still standing ever vigil with his back to the door. The pounding had not lessened in the time he had been gone.

"Well, it is about damn time. What the hell took so long?" Chris asked irritably.

"I had to hit the bathroom. Too many burritos. You understand." Jeff said grinning.

"Of course I understand, as long as you realize that after we take care of this little problem that I will have to use that thing on you. Now, how do we go about doing this?" Chris glanced at the makeshift weapon and silently prayed that it would work.

"I was thinking that you open the door and then fall on the ground. As he tries to eat you, I just hit him in the head." Jeff sounded pleased with his seemingly well thought-out plan, but Chris could not bring himself to share in his enthusiasm.

"Alright, we can call that one 'Plan Shit That Ain't Gonna Happen!'. How about this…" Chris started to lay out a plan that was sure to fail, but had to be better than the "Eat Here" sign that Jeff made up and wanted Chris to hold on his head like a hat.

After a few minutes of debate, Chris was sure of two things. The first being that Jeff wanted him to get eaten and second that he didn't want to be. Finally the plan came together.

"OK." Chris began. "Here's what we are going to do. First you grab that table and bring it over to the door. Then, we will step behind it and as the door opens, we will let the Bloated Bastard come through. Stick with me here. Then we use the table to pin him against a wall and you whack him in the head."

"That could work, but I still think you need the sign." Jeff said laughing nervously. He brought the table over towards the door and moved behind it. "Ready when you are."

"Ready as I can be." Chris gathered his courage for the sprint behind the table and for the psychological trauma that was about to occur.

As soon as Chris took the pressure off of the door, it burst open. He had barely enough time to run to the other side of the table before Jeff began to shove their wooden barrier into the massive zombie, pinning him against the wall next to the door. Instantly Jeff began hitting their former boss in the head, a guttural scream escaping from him, that Chris was sure that Jeff was not even aware he was making. The first blow glanced off of the side, but still managed to cleave a large amount of scalp, sending a spray of blood into the air. Determined to reach his meal, the creature just kept moaning and trying to grab them.

Again and again the weapon fell until, finally, a sickening crack resounded throughout the lobby and their tormenter flattened on the table with a wet thud, his head no longer recognizable. Jeff wrenched the tool free of the matted mess, which sent bits of skull and brain matter flying, and for the second time that day, Chris ruined a potted plant.

"Well." Chris said after he finished. "I guess that's that. At least we are OK. Neither of us were bit. Right?"

Jeff stood staring at the mangled scene before him, shaking slightly at the sight. Unable to speak or tear his eyes from the carnage.

"Dude." Chris said as he slowly approached his friend. "Hey, you alright?" Chris reached over and grabbed Jeff by the arm. This seemed to bring him out of his trance. Jeff turned and raised the weapon as though he were going to hit Chris. Noticing the look of pure shock on Jeff's face, Chris jumped back and just kept trying to talk him down.

"Relax man." Chris pleaded, holding his hands out in a warding gesture. Backing away quickly, he continued to speak in a calming voice. "It's over man. You did what you had to. Remember, we still have to get Janet and get out of here. We can't do that if you are going all Norman Bates on me."

"I just...I..." Was all that Jeff could say as he dropped the bloody tool to the floor. "I killed him."

"No man. Whatever made him a zombie killed him. You just killed a zombie."

"I didn't think it would be like this." Jeff began as he stared into his hands. "I mean, I know what he was and I never liked him in the first place, but to think about killing him and then actually doing it. What is going on here man?" Jeff looked into the face of his friend and for the first time was not sure what to do.

"We still have our original plan. We need to get Janet and get out of the zombie building." Chris said hoping that this would bring Jeff back into reality and ready to get on with their mission. "Now, I need help moving this table so that we can get downstairs. We should head to the security room and look for any other survivors in the monitors. Ready?"

Jeff nodded and, while still looking a little pale, was regaining some of his composure. "There is no way I can be ready for this, but it has to be done, right? By the way, are you sure he is dead?"

"Well." Chris said with a contemplative look. "First, he was technically dead as a zombie and second, he stopped trying to eat us. So I am sure it is safe. Now, grab the end of the table and pull."

Within minutes, they were ready to open the door and head to the security room. The door to the stairwell creaked open and they cautiously peered inside just in case any other creatures were wandering. As they stepped out onto the landing they looked down the flight of stairs and suddenly remembered the other person lying there. It was Levine, the former Vice President of Maverick Cosmetics. Cautiously, the duo descended the stairs.

"You think he is really dead?" Chris asked nervously, maintaining a constant watch on the fallen VP.

"Are they ever?" Jeff replied in an off-handed tone, still feeling the effects of his recent ordeal. "We should just kill him…well kill him again…and be done with it. You want to do this one?" Jeff started to hand the faux machete over to Chris who quickly declined.

"I have a better idea." He said with a slight grin. Chris reached down and grabbed a fallen cinderblock and brought it over his head. "No need to get any closer than we have to right?"

Jeff nodded, still looking slightly pale, and Chris launched the concrete missile down the stairway and missed the now moaning Levine's head, striking him in the back with a stomach-turning crunch. The creature that had been a source of their torment in life was now wailing and trying to pull himself up the stairs to reach the two former guards.

"Great!" Jeff exclaimed. "Now what? You have any more blocks over there?"

"Nope"

"So what, we have to go down there and get within reach. Not loving this plan."

Chris looked at his partner and said, "You do remember it was your plan to come down here looking for Janet right?"

"Details, details. Look, let's just get this over with." Jeff began to creep down the stairs when Chris grabbed his arm. "Why don't we just try throwing other things. There is plenty of debris in the lobby. Let's just grab some and start throwing."

"Fine by me." Jeff said relieved that he would not have to get closer to the advancing horror. "I'll go get something and you wait here."

"Like hell you will." Chris said quickly. "You went for your little knife thing and left me holding the door, now it is my turn to leave you on zombie duty. Besides, if he gets to close you can hit him with your new toy." Looking defeated, Jeff nodded and Chris went to scrounge the lobby for anything heavy.

On his first trip, he managed to bring back a planter that did nothing more than knock the VP down a couple of steps and one of the ruined leather chairs, that just seemed to piss it off.

"You need something heavier." Jeff complained, feeling eager to get away from this thing that kept inching towards him.

"Fine. I have just the thing." Chris hurried into the lobby and returned with their now destroyed television.

"You can't be serious." Jeff said with a look of shock and dismay spreading over his face. "That is almost sacrilege. That little guy has been with us for years. This is how you honor his memory? Heathen!"

"Think of it this way. He has one last hurrah. His final act will be one of kicking ass. It's the way he would have wanted it." Chris said trying to console his friend. Without another word, the television was brought over his head and hurled towards the zombie. With seemingly unerring accuracy, the little projectile struck home and in a shower of gore, ended the miserable existence of Mr. Levine once and for all.

Carefully stepping around the scene at the bottom of the stairs, Chris reached for the door to the first basement level, which had not only Corning's office, but also the office for the lab security team. Carefully they opened the door. Jeff took a cautious look inside as a hand grabbed his shoulder. Screaming and raising the weapon above his head to strike, Jeff turned to find Chris laughing hysterically.

"I just had to do that." Chris said through bouts of laughter. The laughter became less and less as he realized that Jeff had not yet lowered the blade or the hand clutching his heart. "Oh, get that pissed off look off of your face. You would have done the same thing. Trust me, later you'll think this was funny. Now move your ass and get to the security room."

Chris shoved Jeff through the doorway and they began the relatively short walk to the security room. Seeing as how it was right across from the cafeteria, it wasn't hard for them to find.

"Wait a minute." Chris said as he stopped at the door of their destination. "Don't you think I should have some kind of weapon too? I mean having one weapon in a place that has people trying to eat us is just not smart."

"OK." Jeff began as he looked around for something that could be used. "I don't see anything here, but there is a supply closet at the end of this hall or the security team barracks. Which one do you want to?"

"OK, so my choices are the office supplies where we might find another nifty paper cutting thing, or chance a room full of armed zombies. Hmm, let me think about that one. On one hand we have almost no chance of finding a weapon. However, on the other, there may be weapons in there, but in the hands of the un-freaking-dead. I choose option A."

"All right, but a few guns would not hurt right now. That was all I was saying. If you are afraid of a few little zombies, far be it from me to think less of you." Jeff teased as he walked to the supply closet.

The room was thankfully empty and free of the recently deceased; however the only thing that even came close to a weapon was a stapler. Not very useful.

"Alright, new plan." Chris stated as he finally gave up on finding anything to protect himself with. "Here is what we do. We go into the security room. Look at the monitors and see if anything is in the barracks. If not, then we go in. If there is, then we look elsewhere. Sound good?"

"Works for me. Lead on." With that, they headed out to the security room to plan the next stage of their adventure.

They arrived at the door and as Chris was about to open it, Jeff stopped him. "What if there is one in here? Don't you think it would be smart if we knew they were there first?"

"Good idea." Chris agreed. "Here is what we are going to do. You put your ear to the door and see if you hear anything. I will pound on the walls and try to get anything in there to move."

"Not really loving the part with my head against the door." Jeff complained, but he placed his ear against the wooden door. "I don't hear anything. Start pounding."

For the next minute or two they would pound and listen. Finally satisfied that nothing was in the room, they reached for the door when Jeff said, "At least we know that there are no more of them on this level. That racket would have brought them right too us."

"And you only mention this now!" Chris yelled. "Why didn't you say something before we started it? What if they just haven't gotten here yet? Get your ass in there and turn the lights on. I don't want to be out here anymore. Damn jinx. You know that just by saying that, there will be at least one of them that is going to jump out at us now, don't you?"

"Calm down ya sissy." Jeff said grinning, but secretly he wondered himself if he didn't just curse them.

The room was thankfully empty and the monitors were all functioning except for a few in the generator room and two of them on the laboratory level. As their eyes adjusted to the light in the room, they began searching for anything of use. Sadly, the room was the picture of bare. Only the most basic of items were in there. Pens, tablets and flashlights were all that they could find.

Jeff spotted what would hopefully be their salvation sitting on the desk in front of him. He reached over and picked up the phone, intent on calling in everyone from the local police to the Marines. He placed the phone back down and cursed when he realized that there was no dial tone.

They moved towards the bank of monitors and began cycling through them in the hopes of not only locating the one for the sleeping quarters next door, but most importantly for Janet. Minutes passed like hours as they scanned the screens. Hope began to fade, when they suddenly came upon the one for the barracks next door.

Finding the room zombie free, they decided that their best course of action would be to search the room. Gathering their courage and getting ready to leave the relative safety of the security room, they reached for the door handle and carefully opened it. As the door swung aside, both men jumped back in surprise and screamed as a figure fell in upon them. Jeff raised his weapon as the arms of the intruder became entangled in his own.

"Wait!" Chris screamed at the sight of the person seemingly attacking Jeff. "It's Janet."

Jeff pushed himself away and Janet fell to the floor. Staring in shock at the figure before him, he couldn't find his breath. Janet looked up at them and said, "Is that any way to say hello?"

"You're alive!" Jeff was beaming as he pulled her from the hard floor and wrapped her in an embrace. The look of shock and the bulging of her eyes told Chris that she was becoming seriously deprived of oxygen. Pulling Janet away, they looked at her and when they could finally speak, Jeff asked, "What happened down there? How did you get here?"

After replenishing her much needed breath, Janet looked at them both and said, "As far as what happened, that is something I have no idea about. Now how I got here is an interesting story. I was in the waiting area downstairs…"

CHAPTER 6:

A FRIEND

Janet stood staring at the horrific figure before her. Reacting and relying on instinct to get her out of this situation, she shoved the blood-soaked creature as hard as she could. It stumbled and fell on top of another of her colleagues that was beginning to rise.

The door to the staff lounge was almost broken through and Janet frantically began looking for a way out. The man under the fluorescent lamp had begun to free himself and her would be friend was almost on her feet. Wailing monsters were dragging themselves through the hole made in the door; oblivious to the damage they were doing to themselves.

That was when she saw her salvation. Without a moment's pause, she ran towards the opposite side of the room and reached for the loose vent cover that was on the wall. Hauling herself up with strength, speed and determination born from pure, unadulterated fright, Janet managed to get herself mostly into the air duct. That was when the hand grabbed her by the ankle.

Janet did not know or care to whom the hand belonged, she just thrust her feet out with such force that she caught the creature in the jaw and sent it flying back into the group that had finally burst through the now demolished doorway. The last sounds she heard as she entered the ductwork were the terrible moans of the damned and a faint voice asking what was happening.

Sobbing, Janet finished her story. "So I went through the vents and into the supply room next door. I ran from there to the stairs around the corner. I left him." She broke down into tears and collapsed once more upon the floor mumbling about her fault in the man's terrible fate. Her words were hard to make out through the grief. Her shaking form lay curled on the dirty floor.

The guys did their best to make her understand that she hadn't known anyone was still in there and even if she had gone back, there was nothing that she could have done, but these words fell on deaf ears. No amount of consoling was going to ever relieve her of the burden she now felt.

After placing Janet in a chair so that she would be as comfortable as possible, Chris pulled Jeff aside and said, "Look, I am glad we found her and all, but we still have that pesky problem of not being able to leave. Plus, I still have nothing to defend myself with." Noticing the admonishing look written all over Jeff's face, Chris quickly added, "You might think I am being insensitive to her, but let's be realistic here. We are in a damaged building with zombies. We are not going to make it out of here without weapons of some kind. I want to borrow your big blade there and head on over to the security team's room."

Reluctantly, Jeff handed over the weapon as he realized his partner was right. "You can't go over there alone. I need to come with you."

Seeing the concern on Jeff's face, Chris said, "Look, I appreciate your concern, but right now she needs someone to watch her and make sure she doesn't go running back to that room in some foolish attempt to clear her conscience. You are the obvious choice to stay here. She knows you a lot better than she does me and you would have a better chance at restraining her if she becomes hysterical. I also would not mind if you kept an eye on the monitor in case something slips in behind me. Lock the door when I leave and don't open it unless it is me."

"How will I know it's you pounding on the door and not one of those things?" Jeff asked as he resigned himself to the facts of the situation.

"Would one of them yell, 'Open the door and let me in dickhead'? I didn't think so." With that Chris gathered the blade and with a last look at the monitor to make sure that the room was clear, he grabbed a flashlight and left his safe haven and ventured into the unknown realizing that this may be the last he sees of either of them. *I really should have called in sick today.*

Chris made his way to the security team's sleeping area and glanced around the hall before placing his ear to the door to make sure that it was empty. Hefting the blade in his hand and feeling more confident because of it, he grabbed the handle and slowly inched the door open.

Certain that the area was clear, he reached a hand in and began groping for a light switch. After a short time, he found one but the room stayed as dark as it had when he entered. It seems that the few lights in the room were damaged when the building shook.

Chris brought his flashlight up and flicked the switch to on, silently praying for a miracle that it still worked. The tight beam played across the scene in front of him. The room was a picture of military precision, aside from the dust and trash that fell after the building shook. Beds were neatly made and each had a footlocker at the end of them. At the far side of the room sat a small grouping of desks whose contents, while once neatly piled and surely categorized, were now thrown on the floor in complete disarray.

Not willing to let his guard down for a moment, Chris shut the door behind him and made sure that it was firmly closed.

Gathering the courage he did not truly feel, he began to approach the first set of beds, making sure to check the surrounding area just in case one of the monsters were lying on the floor waiting for some poor soul to walk past. Confident that the immediate area was clear, Chris went and began to open the first trunk.

He reached for the latch only to find it locked with a padlock. Glancing behind himself, Chris saw that the other one was locked the same way. *I guess they don't trust each other all that much.* Chris thought as he began to think of a way to open the footlockers. *I could just smash the locks with this blade, but what if it breaks, then not only do we not get anything new to use but we lose the one weapon we had. Maybe the desks will have something.*

Carefully making his way to the opposite end of the room, checking beside every set of beds as he went, Chris came to the first of the 3 desks. Nothing out in the open except a pen and what appeared to be a logbook. Reaching for the high-backed leather chair, Chris shoved out of his way so that he could have a better view of the contents of the desk.

As the chair spun, a hand flew towards him and the bloody face and uniform of one of the guards streaked through his flashlight. Chris had time to scream and take a single step backwards where he slipped on the paperwork that littered the floor; his weapon flew from his hand and slid underneath one of the nearby beds.

Cheitan sat alone in his sanctuary on the bottom-most floor of Maverick Cosmetics, symbols of power and protection carved into the very walls surrounding sparsely furnished room. A carefully drawn circle covered most of the floor. Having been lost in deep meditation for quite some time, Cheitan began to feel stronger and more refreshed. *Soon the time will be right for me to make my presence felt and then none will be able to withstand my onslaught. Without these symbols, I would not have been able to remain hidden for so long. It would simply not bode well if they found out what was happening before my dream has been realized.*

Cheitan opened his eyes and began to allow himself to feel his surroundings. He could sense Mr. Salvin still in his office, which was right where he was meant to be. However he also sensed something he did not expect, others still alive. "How interesting. It could be fun to watch them and see how long they last against my brethren. I can't wait to see how long they live in this first portion of my new kingdom."

Chris scrambled backwards in an effort to put as much distance between himself and the hideous figure before him. As it fell to the floor, Chris noticed that it wasn't moving. More importantly, the dead man's hand held a pistol.

"Well," Chris said beaming as he allowed his heart to slow from the experience, "maybe someone upstairs is looking down and wants us to get out of this shit-hole."

He cautiously approached the fallen figure and hit it once in the head with the heavy blade just to make sure it would not reach for him. *You can never be too careful.*

When he was finally able to tell himself that it was safe, he reached down and picked up the handgun. Ejecting the magazine, Chris noted that it still had an almost full clip. He then proceeded to search the man for any other ammunition. Finding none, he went about searching the desk. While he found nothing that could be used as a weapon, he did notice the journal placed on the desk. An unsteady hand had written:

Not sure what is going on. We got a call to head to the labs. Standard procedure really. Making sure that none of the guinea pigs got out of hand. I sent a team of 4 down there. Never had much trouble before.

Everything was fine until the damn roof fell on us. I immediately dispatched everyone except Rogers and myself to the holding cells just in case. You learn to never be too careful in this line of work.

We were told that everything was under control and the lab rats were still in their cages. I told the team to report back here as soon as possible so that we could work out a plan to deal with this new situation. Rogers said he wanted to go downstairs and help out. Then it happened.

As he opened the door to leave, he just started screaming about his guts being on fire. I never heard anything like that, and I have seen shit that would scare Charles Manson. He fell to the floor and was, I can't even believe I am writing this, crying blood. I mean it was coming out like a faucet. That isn't the strangest thing. I went to help him and the fucking bastard bit me! Took a piece right out of me!

He started to get up and he reached for me. God save me, I could still see the piece of my arm hanging from is mouth. I don't know what I was thinking, but I ran straight at him and kicked him through the door. Once he was through, I shut that bitch as fast as I could, got my gun from my top of my desk and tried to contact the rest of the team. No one answered. I have to assume that either they are dead or still fighting.

Before now, I would not have believed anything like this was possible, but I can feel the pain starting to grow. I know I don't have much time left. I was never what some would call and honorable man, but I do not want to be one of those things. This is probably my punishment for the evil I have done. I can't say I don't deserve it, but I just hope that God will forgive me for the horrors I have committed and for what I am about to do. Goodbye and I hope that someone gets the prick that started this.

Chris put the logbook back on the desk and stared at the man lying before him. He had become used to the thought of zombies by now, but to have read this man's last thoughts brought a sense of realism to the situation that he had not been expecting. Sure the guy was no saint and may have even deserved death, but Chris could think of none that deserved the fate he had endured.

Feeling more confident with the gun in his hand, Chris decided to go back and get Jeff to come help him with the rest of the search.

The guys finished searching the barracks as Janet sat on one of the beds. After seemingly hours of looking through those trunks, which in fact had only been fifteen minutes, they had not found a single round of ammunition. They had, however, managed to reduce the damage to their faux machete by using the blunt end and only going for the weaker looking locks.

Distressed at the fruitlessness of their search, Chris said, "Well, now what are we going to do? We have almost nothing in the way of defending ourselves and we still need to get out of here."

Jeff tried to sound encouraging when he said, "Look at it this way, we had no weapons when we started and we managed to survive so far. Janet had none and she made it out of a room full of those things. We now know

95

that the gates can't be opened from the security room, so that plan is out. We have to get them open and get out. That plan hasn't changed."

"Do you know anyone that can open them?" Chris asked hoping that Jeff knew.

"Not a damn clue." He said.

'I may have an idea." Came a small voice from the front of the room. Janet had gotten off of the bed and seemed to be in somewhat better spirits. Still shaking slightly, she walked back to the guys and continued, "I saw that Dr. Faustus had locked his lab. Maybe he locked this place down too."

"Isn't he that runty doofus that asked us if we wanted a flu shot?" Jeff asked as he turned to Chris.

"Yeah," Chris agreed and he turned to face Janet and said. "We wouldn't get one though. Jeff has that fear of needles and I have that fear of not being able to call in sick."

"Right." Jeff replied. "So you think that he might know how to get out of here? Well, it's the best idea we have, so lets go ask him." And with that, Jeff began walking towards the door, ready to begin the next step that would lead them out of this deathtrap.

"Dude." Chris said as he hurried to catch up. "You do remember that the floor has a zombie horde running around on it? Now I may be wrong, but I seriously doubt that they are there to put on a performance of West Side Story."

"Yeah," Jeff began, but you could see the trepidation beginning to show, "but if this Faustus guy can get us out of Zombie Town USA, then I am all for going down there. We just have to be careful."

"Guys, don't I get a say in this?" Janet asked with an angry look on her face.

"Oh." Jeff started and then thought how best to form his words so that he could leave with both testicles attached. "We just thought that with what happened down there recently, you would be watching us on the monitors."

Chris, knowing that Jeff had said the wrong thing, stepped back and waited for the carnage.

"So what you are saying, " Janet began in a sweet voice meant to disguise the evil she was about to unleash, "is that the poor little girl has to sit and wait for the big strong men to rescue her. Is that it?"

Jeff nodded. The poor fool never knew what hit him.

The floodgates had been opened. "How dare you say that I can't handle myself? In case you have forgotten, I made it out of the entire floor full of zombies and it took the two of you to beat just one of them!" The yelling continued for another few minutes with Chris and Jeff standing there like a deer in headlights unable to move or speak. In the end, they agreed that she should come along and made their way towards the stairs.

A small figure walked into the researchers lounge and stared at the carnage with an intense scrutiny. All around him the feasting of the damned went on. The creatures did not even glance in his direction, but rather they continued to gorge themselves on the flesh of their fellow man. The wailing of these things did not seem to affect him as he took in this ghastly scene.

"I can't believe he has gotten this far so quickly." He said to no one in particular. "He must have been planning this for ages. How has he kept it secret from both sides for so long? I should report this immediately."

He turned and left the room and before he reached the end of the hall, he faded into shadow and was gone.

CHAPTER 7:

INTO THE DEPTHS

Cheitan sat in his sanctuary feeling very confident with the way things were progressing. "They are adapting nicely I think. Soon they will be ready to be released into the world to make my vision become reality at last. Then I can finally be free." He said to himself as he focused upon the things wandering the halls of this steel and concrete tomb. He also noticed that two of his creations were destroyed. Not a great loss, but still, every body counted in this critical stage of his plan.

Suddenly Cheitan's eyes went wide with horror and for the first time in years he knew true fear. *How could they have found out about me? I have been careful. They must have had that little bastard tailing me. Sneaky little fuck. If he tells, then surely nothing could keep me safe. I have to make sure he doesn't return.*

With determination driven by terror at the thought of all of the hard work and effort he has put in becoming pointless, Cheitan quickly set himself to the task of making sure that not a single thing would ever get into his building. Nothing would stop the creation of his new world.

As the trio reached the door to the lab floor, Jeff told Chris that it was his turn to listen for zombies. Reluctantly Chris agreed and placed his head against the cold, steel door.

"I don't hear anything." He said after nearly a full minute of listening.

"Think it's safe?" Jeff asked.

"Only one way to find out." Chris said as he reached for the handle.

"I have an idea." Janet said suddenly. "My lab is right outside this door. If we make a run for it, I think I can get us something to use against those things."

"OK, but whatever we are doing," Jeff said in a hurried tone. "I recommend that we do it quickly. The longer we are here, the more time the Undead Americans in there have to find us."

"Then let's not waste any more time." Chris said. "I for one want to leave this place now." With those final words, he slowly inched open the door, cringing at the seemingly loud squeak that came from the hinges.

That could have gone better. The small man thought to himself as he recounted the report that he had just given. Informing his master of the situation was a job he wished he could have passed on to someone else. The fury that arose from his master would not be held in check. The fact that Cheitan was throwing everything off of balance that could not be tolerated. He was ignoring the rules and that was unacceptable.

He began to fade into the shadows so that he could find Cheitan and deliver proper retribution when suddenly he re-appeared.

"What the Hell?' He said to himself while glancing around for whatever caused this new problem. A sudden look of realization crossed his features as the truth dawned on him. He was locked out. He couldn't get to Cheitan. *The master is not going to like this.* With the knowledge of the punishment he would probably receive for his failure firmly in the front of his mind, he set off to do what needed to be done.

Cheitan sat in his sanctuary. Wincing suddenly, he realized that someone had just tried to enter his new kingdom and failed. Grinning with self-satisfaction that his barrier held, he rose from the cold stone floor. However, Cheitan was no fool. He realized that if given enough time, they would be able to make their way through his hastily constructed wards and then all of the planning he has done for those many years would be for nothing. He would be finished. Tortured for endless eons.

Turning towards the door, he decided to make a trip up to see Mr. Salvin once more. He needed to hurry things along if he was to succeed. The fear of his goal being disrupted firmly entrenched in his mind, Cheitan set off towards the nearest shadow and melted away to appear moments later in the once lavish office of Mr. Salvin.

"How are you doing Alan?" Cheitan asked as he walked towards the now youthful executive. "Have you been keeping yourself busy?"

"Cheitan." Alan said with a start as he noticed the figure emerge from the back of the room. No matter how many times he saw this feat, it still unnerved him. "I was wondering when you would drop by. Are we about through here?"

"Patience." Cheitan said calmly, though he felt his own wearing thin. "It is soon time to end this."

Mr. Salvin got up from his desk and began to pace the room, stepping around the collection of antiques he once held in such high regard, but now were destroyed and lying on the floor. He wasn't sure what made him more nervous; staying here locked in his own building or the way that the dark man stared at him as though he were a prize yet to be claimed. On more than one occasion Cheitan could be caught staring expectantly at him.

Alan felt a strong hand grip his shoulder. "I must leave you now. Take heart knowing that this will all be over in just a few short hours. Until that time, I must insist that you remain here. I will come for you when the time is right."

The now well-known feeling of dread he felt around Cheitan coursed through his body and caused him to shiver. Somehow he had a feeling that this was not going to go according to his plan. Yet, Mr. Alan Salvin, billionaire and owner of Maverick Cosmetics, could do no more than stay in his office and wait for the moment he had once been looking forward to, but now he started to fear.

He stared into the bank of monitors that rested on a small section of his office. He saw the horrors that he had helped to create. He saw the creatures wandering his building, savaging any living thing they fell upon. He recognized more than a few of these faces and felt the familiar regret and sorrow he had felt since this nightmare began. He knew what would happen if he opened the steel shutters that now kept these monstrosities trapped in here. He knew and he wished he could take back what he had done.

Mr. Salvin never deluded himself that his gift would come with a price tag attached and being rich for most of his adult life, he had always been willing and able to pay anything, but as he saw the cost for his youth shambling through the many halls, he realized that his gift was not worth this price. He knew that when he opened those gates, that the world would be paying the price for his youth.

Alan turned his antique leather chair back towards his desk. As he reflected upon the many things in his life and what they had truly meant to him, having been made young again was the one that meant the most. Now though, it felt like a burden. A curse. One which he wished he could take back.

He reached out and opened a small drawer that was concealed in his desk. Reaching inside he pulled out the small .38 caliber pistol he had bought after his first meeting with Cheitan. Six rounds still sat in the chambers, waiting to be unleashed. Dust fell from the barrel as he pulled back the hammer of the gun. Alan had never fired a weapon before, he had never had to, but at close range even he would not miss.

With a final glance in his mirror, he made the decision that he would not be around to watch the folly of his decision unfold. He would not be the one to unleash Hell upon the Earth. Alan Salvin began to utter a prayer for his soul and then, with tears falling from his eyes, he raised the gun to his head.

Chris peeked through the small crack in the door and suppressed a string of curses. "There is one standing right outside. No way can we just get past him."

"So we have to take him out." Jeff said stating the obvious. Jeff stared at the two companions as he realized what they were about to ask him to do. "You have got to be shitting me."

"Look," Chris began in his still whispered tone, constantly checking to make sure the zombie still waited outside the door like a sentry unwilling to give up his post, "if I shoot him, then more will come. Too noisy man. We can't risk it."

Chris saw the look of concern on Jeff's face and did his best to relieve that stress. "He isn't even facing us. If we open the door fast, you have a lot of time before he would even know you were coming. Just run up behind him and take him out."

Barely able to be heard, Jeff whispered, "I can't."

"What do you mean you can't?" Chris asked, barely hiding the frustration he felt. Then he remembered the way that Jeff had reacted when he had to deal with the Corning Zombie and his features softened a little. "Alright. Give me the blade and I will do it."

Jeff handed over the weapon and gave a look of thanks to his friend. Chris nodded and prepared to engage the enemy. A final glance through the crack in the door told them that the thing was still in the same position.

Janet grabbed the door handle and Jeff stood up higher on the steps so that Chris would have room to gain speed for his mad rush. Chris stood and began breathing quickly in order to build up the courage to do what needed to be done. He gave a final glance at Jeff and then looked towards Janet and nodded.

As she flung the door wide, Chris charged for all he was worth at the shambling, moaning creature. As he began to draw near, it slowly started to turn. Chris brought the blade around in a high arc meant to cleave the head of the monster in two. Not everything goes according to plan.

The distance to the thing was only a few feet at best and what Chris had not counted on was a ceiling tile lying on the floor. Once he stepped on it, the ground seemed to come out from under him and he found himself sliding towards the waiting jaws of death.

Janet saw the scene unfolding in seemingly slow motion. She screamed for Jeff and ran to help her fallen friend. Jeff was beside her in an instant, having watched the scene unfold as well. Gathering as much speed as possible, Jeff ran forward and launched a devastating kick at the creature's mid-section. The impact sent the thing flying backwards before it had time to reach for the group.

Chris pulled himself from the floor, dusting off his clothes and cursing his bad luck as he picked up the blade. A determined and angry look crossed his face as he stalked towards the fallen zombie. A cry from behind him caused a momentary pause in his pursuit. He turned to look down the hall and noticed the mass of living dead shuffling towards them.

"Janet, get that damn lab open now!" Chris yelled as he prepared to make the rush inside. Constantly throwing whatever he could find at the approaching multitude. His improvised projectiles doing little more than causing them to stumble over each other as the pieces of debris collided with them.

Janet ran towards the keypad beside her lab door and began entering the code. More than once she had to start over, cursing herself and inwardly questioning if they could make it out of this nightmare.

We can always make a run for the door and just find another way down. She tried again and finally, as the creatures drew ever nearer, she got it right. The door was opened quickly and they hurried inside. Slamming the door as the first zombie scraped the window with a blood soaked hand. A sudden realization came across each of them as they stared awestruck out the window at the collection of people. They were trapped.

CHAPTER 8:

CHOICES

Cheitan was getting nervous. He could scarcely afford to have any complications creating delays for his plans. Having just left Salvin's office, he was pacing the gore-covered halls when he found himself wandering towards the large mass of creatures near the break-room. As he walked among them and he felt a sense of pride at what he had accomplished. He stared at what he had come to think of as his family with pride.

He could feel his plans coming together and he sensed that the time for stealth would be over shortly. Soon everyone would know and nothing could stop him then. They would try of course.

Suddenly a loud crash was heard from behind him. He turned to see a man rushing at one of his brothers swinging a large weapon. He watched the comical scene as he fell and was only moments away from becoming his newest brother. That was when the other one showed and interrupted the feast.

Disappointed at the denial of the show, Cheitan, unwilling to reveal himself to others, disappeared into shadow. He found himself back in the office of Alan Salvin ready to tell the man of the things he had just seen, eager to know who fought against him. Not that he was concerned, just curious. When for the second time this day, Cheitan knew true fear for sitting behind a large desk was one Alan Salvin with a gun pointed at his head.

Temporarily stunned by the image before him, Cheitan almost did not react in time. Raising one mighty hand towards the suicidal Salvin, Cheitan caused the air before him to ripple like the asphalt on the hottest days of summer. Suddenly Mr. Salvin screamed in agony and the gun clattered to the floor. The crosshatch pattern of the pistol's grip was seared into his hand.

Cheitan watched as the man fell to the floor, screaming in agony, but still reaching for the weapon. He quickly crossed the room, went behind the desk and bent down to retrieve the pistol from its resting place on the floor. Utter contempt and disgust lined his features as Cheitan lifted the newly young Mr. Salvin from the floor and unceremoniously dumped him back into his chair.

With a calm voice that hid none of the malice he felt, Cheitan glared daggers at Salvin and said, "What do you think you were going to do with this?" He held up the confiscated weapon and continued to hold Mr. Salvin in his piercing gaze.

Defiantly, Alan Salvin pulled himself into his chair so that he sat with some of the pride he used to feel. He stared into the hate filled eyes of Cheitan, whom he once considered a partner, and said, "I plan to end this miserable existence. I know what I have done to those people out there and I just hope that I can be forgiven. I can't take this anymore. I want it over."

Tears welled up in the mans eyes as he once again recalled the images he has seen over the last few hours and the horrors he has helped to commit against those brought in for the research. "I have much to atone for. I can't even begin to pay for my sins, but I can't add more to them. I want you to take back your gift. I want to make things right."

A deep guttural laugh escaped from Cheitan. "Take it back? I can't believe what I am hearing. For years you have schemed and plotted to bring in people to die in your labs," then all humor left Cheitan's face as he screamed, "and now you develop a fucking conscience!"

In a fit of pure rage, Cheitan threw the pistol to the back of the room and stalked towards the cowering Salvin. Salvin felt the powerful grip tighten around his throat as he was lifted from his chair and brought to within inches of the anger filled eyes of Cheitan.

"You want death?" Cheitan asked as a smile played across his features that held no humor within it. "I will show you death." With those words Alan Salvin knew that his time upon this Earth was almost at an end, but not before Cheitan was finished with him.

Fear threatened to overtake them all as they stared into the throng of undead gathered outside the laboratory scratching and clawing to get inside. The faces of their tormenters contorted in hunger, just eager to reach their next meal. Ready and willing to rend flesh and taste hot blood flowing down their throat. Smears of red had increased on the large window that overlooked the hall as many hands ran along it. Mouths open in anticipation, the sounds unheard in the lab thanks to the thick shatterproof windows. Although the creatures could not gain entry, their relentless attack on the small safe haven would not end.

"We are officially screwed." Jeff said softly as he stared at the sight in front of him. Unable to tear his gaze away from the images that he knew would haunt him for the rest of his days, no matter how long they may be.

"Not yet we aren't." Chris said more to calm his own quickly failing nerve than anything else. "All we have to do is stick to the plan of getting out of here. Then we can call the Army and they can deal with this."

Sweat beading on his brow, Jeff was stunned at his friend's simple explanation of the situation. "Sounds easy in theory. How exactly do you plan on getting us out of here?"

"Haven't quite worked that out yet." Chris said, never taking his eyes off of the window and the event unfolding outside. He knew the chances were slim of them surviving, but he also knew that they had to. Nothing else really mattered. They could do nothing for the poor souls that have already been turned, but they had to save themselves.

Realizing that Janet had not yet said anything, the guys turned to her to make sure that she had not had another breakdown. Her blank eyes seemed focused on empty space, as she just stood there unmoving.

"Hey," Jeff began. "I think we need to close those shades. We can't hear them, but that is really starting to creep me out." He pointed to the large retractable blinds located above the large window.

"While I hate the idea of not knowing what they are up to, I can't stand the sight of them either." Chris admitted. "Do you want to close them or should I?"

"Please," Jeff said with a grin. "Be my guest." With a wave and a deep bow, he gestured towards the blinds indicating that Chris could have all of the fun that came along with going close to the creatures with nothing but the pane of glass between them.

Quickly regretting his offer, Chris set off slowly to perform the task that would conceal the things from their view and allow them to get on with the more important mission of getting out of the building. As he drew nearer, the activity outside intensified. The clawing of the window grew more forceful and the moans reached a new level of intensity, which was only evident by the widening of the creatures' jaw. It was as if they knew that food was close enough to devour, but remained out of reach.

Carefully, as though he were afraid that the glass would shatter at any second, Chris reached up and drew the blinds down; effectively cutting the horrific display from their view. This seemed to bring Janet out of her state of shock. As she slowly began recovering, she said a word of thanks to Chris for what he had just done.

"So what's the plan?" asked Chris, as he grew more relaxed and noticed the others do the same.

"First thing is first." Janet said quickly, regaining more of her composure every second. "We need more weapons. We should be able to find something in here that can help us out. Then we just need to get to Faustus so that he can open these shutters."

Unable to deny the logic of the plan, the guys agreed and set themselves to the task of searching the laboratory for anything usable for defense.

Shelves were lined with chemicals and small glass vials. Cabinets housed more of the same.

After a few minutes of pointless searching, Janet said, "Sorry guys. I thought for sure that there would have been something in here we could use. We still have to check my office and the supply closet."

Jeff volunteered himself and Chris to search the closet while Janet, who would know the place better, checked her office. They walked over to the doorway to the small office, confident that they would find nothing un-living inside, and opened the door.

As certain as they seemed, a sigh of relief escaped from their collective lips as they found the room empty of anything hostile. Assured that the area was safe, Chris and Jeff left Janet to search her office and proceeded to their destination.

Jeff grabbed the doorknob and opened the door to the supply room. This one was much larger than the last one. Housing more than simple office supplies, it also contained the chemicals and equipment that the staff would require and having it located in the lab meant less downtime searching for materials necessary for the completion of their work.

Now, however, the room was in shambles. File cabinets overturned and glass shattered on the floor spilling chemicals. And at the opposite end of this once pristine and orderly area was a lone figure. Taking in the pallid features of the man sitting on the floor, both men made ready to defend themselves.

Chris raised his gun to fire on the thing before him and quickly told Jeff, "You need to let Janet know what was happening. I can handle this one. Besides, I have Betty."

"Tell me you did not name the gun." Jeff said as he cast a sidelong glance at Chris, never taking his full attention away from the seated body.

"What's wrong with Betty?"

"Nothing is wrong with the name Betty. What is disturbing is that you would name the gun." Jeff said. "Only those of the insane variety do that and if you are going loony, I think you should give me the gun."

"You keep your dirty hands off of Betty. Just go let Janet know what is happening." Chris said finally and Jeff went to inform Janet of the situation.

Realizing that his aim with the pistol was somewhere above the abysmal range, Chris decided that he should try and get a little closer so that he could make all of his shots last. His ammunition was limited and he had no guarantees of finding any other rounds. So ever so slowly he crept closer to the unmoving form. Glass crunched under his feet as he stepped on a vial that lay on the floor. Wincing at the noise he decided that he had come far enough and would no longer be able to risk coming within reach of the zombie.

Chris raised the gun to eye level, careful to hold it at arms length with his elbows slightly bent like he had seen in dozens of movies. He took aim at the only thing truly visible, the top of the head. Breathing in deeply to settle his nerves and in hopes of keeping his hand steady he slowly squeezed the trigger. And nothing happened.

"Damn it!" he cursed to himself as he reached for the safety on the gun. Once again he brought the pistol up and aimed. As he prepared to fire, something caused him to stop.

Unsure if his senses were playing tricks on his tired mind, Chris listened harder. Sure enough he heard a faint voice coming from the zombie. But they couldn't talk. Could they?

But surely, there it was again. "Help me."

The voice was weak and trembling. Between shallow breaths the man said, "Not...one...of them"

Quickly Chris called for help and Jeff came rushing into the room ready to smite whatever was threatening his friend. When he saw Chris at the back of the room helping the thing to its feet, Jeff stood in surprise.

"Its alright, " Chris began quickly. "He's alive. Help me get him into the office."

Between the two of them they managed to get the man seated into Janet's chair. They did their best to make him comfortable as he thanked them for helping him.

"Not sure how much longer I could have stayed in there." He said through ragged breaths. The simple act of talking seemed to sap what little strength the man had remaining. He slumped lower in the seat and it looked as though he were about to drift off to sleep, when he suddenly gripped the arms of the chair and forced himself upright with a strength that seemed to come from sheer desperation. The toll this simple act had on him was evident through the grimace spreading across his face.

Janet moved closer to him. Not sure what exactly she intended to do for this man's suffering, she was not a medical doctor, Janet reached for the man's hand.

The stranger looked at each of them in turn. A defeated expression reached the already haggard looking face as he drew a deep breath. He asked the assembled trio to have a seat because he had something important to say. Then he told his story.

"My name is William Harris. I was one of the private security team hired to guard the lab areas. We were sent down here to take our usual positions outside the lab." He began as he returned to the relative comfort of the office chair. "I was watching what was going on inside the lab through those large windows they have. I saw that doctor walking around one of the lab tables and talking to the guy they had on there."

He paused to collect both his strength and his thoughts. His brow furrowed and his expression grew into anger as he recounted the next few minutes. "You couldn't hear anything with the glass being so thick, but just seeing that poor bastard lying there, bleeding out. I thought he was dead for sure. Then all of a sudden the guy just gets off of the table smiling like nothing was wrong. Strangest thing I had ever seen."

A grin played across his face that held no humor behind it. "Funny really. Strange just went right out the fucking window about two minutes later."

Running his hands through his sweat soaked hair; he lowered his head as though he had fallen asleep. A scant few seconds had passed, when he raised it once more. He looked more determined than ever to finish his tale, his voice still ragged but it seemed much stronger.

"We saw the guy walking to the door. Then he got this look on his face. Hard to describe unless you have seen someone in extreme pain. Then he just dropped. We got the order to go in and secure the situation. The first thing that hit us as we opened that door was the screams. I have been in countries where war was as common as breakfast, but never were there screams like this." Suddenly overcome by a fit of violent coughing, William fought hard to compose himself. Janet rose to lend him as much help as she was able, but he waved her back into her seat. "I need to finish this."

Drawing in as much air as he could he continued, "Someone ordered us to take him back to the holding area. None of us wanted to touch him, so we grabbed a wheelchair and a couple of the guys put him in there. We took him back and put him in his cell. Then the hole place went to Hell."

"Me and the guys were just putting the guy into bed when the whole damn place just started shaking and the next thing I knew the rest of the team showed up. We secured the area and soon after that the lights came back on. We took a few minutes to get our shit together and then went downstairs to see if there was any major damage to the place. We saw that fat guy waddling up the stairs. We had more important things to do than worry about him though." Chris and Jeff exchanged a look and were about to tell William just what happened to Corning, but decided to wait until he was finished.

"We got to the basement level and were talking about how we were going to straighten this shit out when just suddenly half the team was acting just like that guy from the lab." He looked around the room at nothing in particular as if searching for a way to get rid of these memories. His gaze fell back upon his audience and he regained his composure.

"They died. They were dead and the only thing I could think of was that I was glad I wouldn't have to hear their screams. Gene, Alex, James, Davis, and Michaels were all dead in a matter of minutes. Ford decided to go over and check their pulse for some damn reason. Clear as day that they were dead."

True fear had begun to show itself on William's face as he continued his tale. When he spoke it was clear that he was no longer talking to anyone in the room.

"He reached down to feel for a pulse and Gene just reached out and bit him. Just like that. I pulled Ford back and as the rest of us stood back, the others stood up. I fired a few shots into Gene, but he just kept on coming. Constantly moaning. Reaching for us. A few more shots from the others. Nothing. We ran to the stairs firing as we went."

"Then the door to the janitor's room flew open and he came right at me. No time to dodge, I just threw my arms up." He looked down at his blood soaked sleeve and the group knew what had happened. "I broke his neck and he fell. We hauled ass out of that place. We split up after that. Not sure what happened to the rest of them."

Again a fit of uncontrollable coughing came over William. He brought himself to his feet as he stumbled towards the exit to the small office. He collapsed on the tiled floor outside the office. A look of sudden terror came over him as he looked at the faces of Chris, Jeff and Janet. He knew what was coming and he knew that they had come to the same conclusion.

"You have to do it." William said calmly as he took in their faces. "I know what's happening. I am becoming one of them ain't I?" He needed no answer. The truth was plain to see.

"We can't be sure," Janet began.

"Don't try to bullshit me!" William screamed, spitting blood on the floor. Jeff noticed it too. The small trickle of blood forming at the side of his mouth and the pale skin meant one thing. He was turning. He wouldn't go out that way.

Pain wracked his body in ever intensifying waves. He started screaming and realized where he had heard those sounds before. His every muscle began to cramp and stiffen, not even allowing himself the luxury of putting a bullet into his own head. Finally, with an ultimate surge of great will, he managed to get out two words, "Kill me."

Chris and Jeff exchanged looks and knew what had to be done. They would want the same if they were in his position. As they looked into the pleading eyes of the dying man, Chris drew his gun.

CHAPTER 9:

FIRST CONTACT

Jeff and Janet stared blankly at Chris, words failing them at the moment. What was witnessed in that laboratory would haunt them forever.

Janet had been protesting what she knew was about to happen. She felt strongly that there might be a way to save the suffering man lying in a pool of his own blood that was growing steadily larger. The pleading look in William's eyes had made the decision much easier, but Chris would be the one that would have to live with it. Killing the dead was one thing; this was murder.

William begged and screamed for death and still Janet attempted to stop what was unavoidable. Chris slowly brought his weapon up and as he cocked the hammer with trembling hands, William said, "Thank… you."

Janet turned her face into Jeff's chest and covered her ears so she would not bear witness to the scene a few feet from her. Still she heard the muffled sound of the gun's report echoing and the silence that followed.

William laid still, his last request granted. He would not rise again.

He walked with a purpose. Determination etched across the evil smile Cheitan wore as he pulled the struggling man behind him. Up the long hall towards the mass of living dead wandering outside a laboratory as though something they deeply desired was inside if only they could reach it.

"Here Alan," Cheitan began with a wide, sweeping gesture. "This is the price for your youth. Quite different from what you have been watching on your little monitors in the office isn't it?" With that he threw Alan Salvin roughly at the feet of the creatures like a master throwing his dogs a bone to fight over. However, before the first creature reached the humiliated and sobbing Salvin, Cheitan quickly came up from behind and lifted him into the air.

Holding him just out of the reach of the moaning undead, Cheitan said still wearing the grin he had not lost since he first started walking towards the mass of living dead intent on instilling more than just simple fear into Alan, "Is this a close enough look at death for you? Should I let them have a little taste?" Deep-throated laughter issued from Cheitan as he toyed with his captive. Cold, dead hands reached for him and tried to draw him nearer to their hungry maws.

Alan Salvin screamed as they managed to grab his shirt. Shock and terror ran through him as he lost all control of his bladder. "Please." He begged as he tried to kick away the rotted, blood stained hands that grabbed for him. "Don't do this."

"Oh, don't worry poor, pathetic Alan." Cheitan said as he hoisted Alan higher out of their reach. "I have much grander plans for you."

Cheitan then turned, still holding Salvin in the air, and began to walk back towards the office that Alan now realized was more of a prison than his old age had ever been. He took a final glance back at the swarm of monsters and saw them hungrily following in their slow, loping gait, reaching for him and constantly emitting their moaning wail. But Cheitan did not open the large wooden doors that lead to Salvin's office. Instead Cheitan placed Alan on his massive shoulder like someone carrying a sack of grain and together they went for the stairs. As they descended, Alan saw that a few of the shambling creatures had managed to make their way through the doorway and were now stumbling, and in some cases falling, down the stairs. It would have been comical if not for the fact that Alan knew he was probably going to join them soon in death.

When they arrived in the basement only moments later, Cheitan went to one of the rooms near the back and opened the thick metal door. The room inside smelled of mold and dampness. Alan was roughly thrown into a chair located in the far corner of the room, which toppled over, spilling him on the floor. He righted himself and stared at the pacing Cheitan wondering just when he would finally get to leave this horrid existence behind. Salvin took in his surroundings, noting the strange symbols on the wall and a lack of any other furniture in the room.

"I am sure that you are wondering why you were not fed to my brothers." Cheitan said without even bothering to look in Salvin's direction. "That is quite a long story."

"I can't believe I made it out of there still in one piece." The short figure said as he walked back to the area where he last attempted to enter the domain of Chetian, thinking of his encounter with his master. He still felt the barriers blocking his entry and no matter how he tried, he still could not gain access. "Even more unbelievable is how he was able to get to Earth at all. He should not be able to. Only the strongest among us can visit that wretched place and even if we do manage to get topside, we are not allowed to interfere with them. Influence only. That was the first rule. If he is planning what I think he is, then he is even more foolish than I thought."

He readied himself to project as much of his senses as he could into the building, hoping to find something he could use to stop Cheitan. A sudden surge ran through his body as he felt someone experiencing a violent end.

Searching for the source, he had found his way inside. He just might be able to stop Cheitan and keep the other side from ever finding out. He sat on the ground and crossed his legs. Pouring all that he possessed into the deep concentration that his solution required. He shut his eyes and focused everything he had on the one who had just entered his domain. He found what he needed.

Even after regaining her composure, Janet could still not bring herself to look Chris in the eye. She kept her gaze towards the floor unless she was speaking to Jeff. They had agreed that they needed to find a way out of the lab. Not an easy feat when there were undead stationed outside the door just waiting for an easy lunch.

"We can go though the air vents like I did." Janet suggested.

"Maybe you two can." Jeff said as, for the first time, he regretted his size.

"Shooting them is out. Even with the gun I found on William," Chris paused as he saw Janet wince at the mention of the man's name. "There are just not enough shots. We need another way."

Chris noticed Jeff looking around the room as though he was searching for something.

"Do you smell that?" Jeff asked wrinkling his nose at the odd odor that seemed to be filling the room.

"Well I didn't before you said anything. Next time warn people so that they can cover their faces." Chris said while waving a hand in front of his face.

"Wasn't me that time. Smells like something is burning."

They all quickly began looking around for any signs of smoke or fire, when suddenly Janet knelt down by the fallen William. She went completely pale. Gasping for breath, she stumbled backwards away from the strange occurrence before them. William's blood, which was spreading in an ever-increasing puddle over the floor, had begun to steam. Small bubbles began forming within the red liquid. Slowly, but deliberately, those bubbles coalesced into words.

Disbelief washed over them all as they read *Need a hand?*

They stared open mouthed at the sight in front of them. None of them were quite sure of what they had seen. There were words forming in the man's thickening blood.

Jeff finally broke the eerie silence, "Is this really any stranger than anything else we've seen today? Should I remind you of the cleaning lady Chris?"

"I wish you wouldn't." came his reply. "You guys aren't thinking of trusting whatever this is, are you? I mean dude, it is words written in blood. OK, forget the fact that it is extremely high on the creepy meter, this shit ranks up there with things that the evil guys do to fuck with you. You never hear of good guys writing messages in blood. They use glowing lights or little yellow sticky notes."

"You done ranting yet?" Janet had finally spoken up. "We need a way out and if this whatever is willing to help, we have to at least hear what it has to say."

"She has a point." Jeff said with a look that asked Chris not to start an argument with Janet. "We can just listen, well read, and if he asks us to kill puppies or something equally evil, like watching the Golden Girls, we just say no."

Finding the odds two to one, Chris admitted defeat. "Fine, how do we communicate with it? You want to start making blood bubble art, be my guest. I for one will not be joining in on that past time."

I can hear you. The letters were appearing much faster than before.

"Alright," Chris began skeptically. "You want to help us? How do we get out of here?"

The last message faded with the faint sound of the bubbles popping as new ones rose to take their place. *Safe to run.* Again, the message left.

"Safe to run where?" Janet asked leaning forward to read the answer. When after a full minute none came, she sat back.

"Maybe he doesn't like girls." Jeff said, quickly wishing he couldn't speak as she shot him a glare that could melt steel.

"Obviously he meant it is safe outside. Now we know that is a lie because the last time I looked out there, there was a gaggle of ghouls waiting for their dinner." Chris said triumphantly as he looked towards the still drawn shades.

"Maybe they left," Janet shot back at him. Turning the full glare away from Jeff.

"One way to find out isn't there?" Chris said staring back, frustration beginning to surface. "How about you go have a look?" Chris gestured for her to stand and go to the window.

"Guys, knock it off." Jeff said annoyed at the childish behavior he was witnessing. "I'll go look."

"No!" Janet yelled as she quickly stood. "I can do it." Determined, she walked towards the window. Slowly she grabbed the shade and pulled it down, ready to let the thing retract quickly. Hesitating for a moment, she glanced back and saw the satisfied smug look Chris had given her and all fear left her. She let go and the window was visible again. And the hall was empty.

"There will be no living with her after this." Chris simply said, remembering a quote from Jeff's favorite movie. Jeff grinned. Janet sauntered back to them and picked up the extra gun from the floor.

"You ready to go?" she asked as she turned towards the door.

"Ready to go? Sure, but where are we going to?" Chris called after her.

"The plan still stands. Get the gates up and get out of here." Jeff said as he followed after Janet. "That means we hit Faustus' lab and see if we can't find the switch and finally get out of this nightmare."

"Please Ascaroth," the creature said as he stared into the cold eyes of the small figure standing above him. "No more. I know nothing." Beaten and bloody, the creature raised his hands in order to protect himself, knowing full well that mercy did not exist in either this place or in the figure before him.

"You have told me nothing Bechet. However, that does not mean you know nothing." Cold determination gripped Ascaroth as he grabbed Bechet around the throat, hauling him into a seated position. "You can either tell what you know to me, or you can tell it to him."

Bechet knew full well of whom Ascaroth spoke. He knew that the punishment he now endured would be a pleasure compared to what would come from a meeting with him. He needed no further incentive.

Some time later Ascaroth found himself walking back to the place where his master lived. He recounted the information he had gained. He told of how Cheitan had accomplished his feat. "I would say that what he was doing was not possible had I not felt it within the blood of one of the new arrivals." Ascaroth told his master when he had finally finished his tale. "Such a thing has never been attempted."

"You sound as if you admire this upstart." His master said from the darkened corner in which he sat.

"No sire." Ascaroth quickly said in attempt to escape his master's rage. "I was simply saying that his arrogance is bold."

His master leaned forward out of the darkness and brought himself eye level with Ascaroth. Bright fire burned behind those terrible eyes that promised pain and suffering for all who displeased him.

"He could not have done this alone. Give me the names of those with him and I will see to their fate." The booming voice reverberated throughout the entire area and the one to whom it belonged sat back into the shadows once again. "In the meantime, I will search for the means to put an end to his little uprising and you will make sure that he does not succeed while I am searching."

Janet reached for the doorknob as Jeff watched out the window for anything trying to sneak up on them. They slowly opened the door and peered outside.

"See anything?" Jeff asked as he continued his vigil at the window.

"I see a couple of them outside Faustus' lab. Now what?" She said feeling somewhat defeated.

"We could just run in there with guns blazing, but that plan never works in the movies." Jeff said. He turned to Chris who had not yet joined them near the door. Jeff saw him staring at the man on the floor. He walked back to Chris. Making sure that Janet was still watching the zombies, Jeff whispered to Chris, "You did what none of us could have. It was for the best. I know you would want me to do the same for you."

"Thanks man." Chris said, feeling a little better after hearing the much needed words of encouragement that his long time friend had given him. He looked up and managed a trademark cocky grin as he said, "I still think we should have called in sick today."

Jeff threw and arm over Chris' shoulder and as they walked to the door he said, "And miss all of this fun?"

"Are you ready?" Janet asked anxiously as she glanced back at Chris and Jeff. "We need to hurry before more come."

"Here." Chris said as he handed Janet the extra clip that he had retrieved from William. "Only has a few shots so make them count. Head only. Jeff, do you still have your big knife thingy?"

"Yeah." Jeff said feeling a little defensive about his choice of weaponry.

"Good. We will probably need it if more of them come. Another thing, If we run out of ammo or if there are too many, we run back here. Clear?

Janet nodded and they started down the hallway.

Barely reaching the halfway point between their door and Faustus' lab, the creatures turned as if they had one mind and started slowly coming towards them.

A shot rang out as Chris fired at the closest creature. The shot hit solidly in the wall next to it. "If you are going to shoot like that then I am just going to grab the ketchup from the break room and lather up." Jeff said hoping to piss Chris off enough that he would concentrate harder and forget being nervous as a half-dozen ravenous things marched towards them.

Another shot and a body fell to the floor, slumping right in the path of another that was one the way towards them. Janet grinned in a self-satisfied way as she shot a look over at Chris. "One for me." She said triumphantly.

Grumbling under his breath, Chris took a more careful aim and placed a shot into the eye socket of one of the creatures, sending its brain out the other side of its head. And another had fallen. That left four to contend with.

The gang noticed that the four zombies had not yet reached the entry to Faustus' laboratory. Cautiously, they moved closer in the hopes of making it inside without having to deal with the things.

"Jeff," Chris started. "Go try the door and we can cover you."

Jeff said, "With your shooting, I think I would be safer with the zombies." He hesitantly went closer to the door, grabbed the handle and instinctively ducked as another shot rang out.

"Sorry!" Chris said as plaster rained down on Jeff.

"You know," Jeff yelled as he looked back to see that the progress of the undead had brought them closer to him, but still out of reach. "I think I should just walk over there and let them bite me." He pulled on the door as another of the creatures fell. He heard Janet's mocking laughter as she let Chris know she was ahead in points. He felt his heart nearly stop as the door failed to open.

A loud crack and this time it was Chris who made sure his shot was successful. Jeff turned and counted two of them left and they were getting closer. He could smell the sickly stench of rot coming from them. He decided to get the hell out of there fast.

He ran back to Janet and Chris and told them that the door was locked. "Do you have a code for this one?" Jeff asked Janet as she took careful aim and let another shot fly into the skull of a creature, putting it down for good.

"Nope. Only Faustus has that." She said as she sighted another zombie. "Last one Chris." She pulled the trigger and an empty click echoed throughout the hall.

"Told you there weren't many shots left." Chris said with a self-righteous grin on his face. "Let me get this one." He aimed the pistol carefully, drew in a steadying breath and fired. The thing that had once been a human fell to the floor.

Pleased with himself Chris said, "Let's just go and pound on the window. He will see us and let us in."

"Sounds like a plan." Jeff said and they walked carefully down the hall, listening intently for sounds of shambling or moaning creatures, all the while trying to ignore the sound that their footsteps made in the carpet that was now soaked with the blood of the dead.

Having cleared the immediate vicinity of the undead beings, the gang reached the window that looked into Faustus' lab without any further incident. Their hearts sank as they gazed inside because on the floor they could clearly see the lifeless body of the late Dr. Marlin Faustus.

"OK now what?" Chris asked as he resigned himself to walking back to Janet's lab. He looked at Janet and Jeff in turn, hoping that they could suggest something.

"We could try to get in through the animal pens. There is a door in the back that leads right into his office." Janet suggested as she pointed to a door nearer the stairs. "Or we could try looking in Dr. Faustus' room. He has living quarters here."

Jeff was glancing behind them to make sure that none of the creatures were attempting to sneak up on them. At her suggestion, Jeff replied, "You know him better than we do. If you think he would have something that had the codes just lying around in his room, then we check there."

"Or," Chris began as he looked around cautiously. "We could split up and each check a different place. I mean, what if the door in the back is locked too? Then we would have wasted all that time. But if someone is searching the room while the others are checking the back of the animal pens, we could get two things done at once."

"Chris," Jeff said. "Have you been watching Scooby Doo again? Split up and search for clues huh? I guess that makes us the meddling kids."

Chris threw his hands in the air in a frustrated gesture and said, "If you guys have anything better, let me know."

Jeff started to say something when Janet quickly cut him off. "No, he is right. As much as I would hate to split up, it is the best thing. The faster we search means the faster we get to leave here."

"Janet," Chris said eager to get this nightmare over with. "You will go with Jeff and check out the animal pens. I will go to Faustus' room."

"Hate to break it to you Chris, but you wouldn't really know what to look for in there." Janet said as she prepared to walk down the hall.

"True," Chris said while silently asking Jeff to step in and help deal with her. "But what if there are locks on the animal pens? What if there is something in that lab that can help us find out what caused this? I wouldn't have any idea what I was looking at if it fell in my lap. Now, no more arguments. Let's just get it done."

"Alright," Janet said. "His room is at the end of this hall. Last door on the left." She pointed at the hallway directly across from where they now stood.

Saying final words of encouragement and making sure that they were prepared for whatever they were going to face, the gang went their separate ways.

CHAPTER 10:

SEPARATION ANXIETY

Chris started down the long hallway that would lead him to Faustus' private quarters. Passing a shattered door lying on the floor, he quickly hurried past when he heard no sounds coming from inside. Not eager to go exploring places he wasn't sure of in case they hid something he would rather not meet.

He reached the room without incident. He listened intently at the door for anything lurking within. Not daring to let anything sneak up behind him, he kept looking back up the hall. Assured that the room was at least quiet, Chris reached for the handle. Thankfully the door opened without any problems.

Chris found the light switch by the door and the room became bathed in the soft glow of fluorescent lights. Inside he found the state of the room to be typical of the rest of the building. Papers were scattered on the floor. Items had fallen off of shelves.

Chris took his time in taking in the surroundings, noting where a potential undead could remain hidden. Seeing the room sparsely furnished did nothing to cause him to let his guard down. He carefully checked under the bed and in the lone closet. Nothing had decided to make either place their temporary home.

Seeing a small nightstand beside the bed, Chris decided to check there for anything interesting. He pulled the drawer open and the only item of note was a small book of fairy tales. The cover was worn and the spine showed frequent use. He tossed it back in the drawer and walked towards an area that looked like an office.

He went to a small desk located near the back of the room. On it was all kinds of office supplies. Everything looked fairly standard except for the general condition of the area. It was a complete mess. He started clearing off the area, throwing things that seemed worthless to the floor.

After finding nothing that Chris could say was informative on the top, he began searching through the drawers of the desk. More of the same items littered the inside of these as rested upon the top. Chris had noticed that one of the drawers was locked.

He considered looking for a key to open it and realized that such an effort would take up valuable time. Not to mention that he had no idea where to start looking. Instead, he simply turned the small desk over and reached for the soft underbelly of the drawer.

A few loud bangs later, Chris had kicked in the bottom and its contents spilled out for him to inspect. The small drawer contained only two things, both of which were snatched up by Chris. The first was a large roll of money. *He won't be needing this anymore.* Chris said to himself as he was faced with the dilemma of sharing his newfound wealth with Jeff. The second was a wire-bound journal. In it were complicated notes on chemicals and experiments that Chris had no chance of deciphering. He decided to make sure that Janet could take a look at his findings, well the second of his findings at least.

He continued his search for a way to open the steel plates that covered the doors and windows. When he found nothing he decided to end his search and meet up with the others. But first, Chris went over to the small mini-fridge to see if the doctor had anything to drink. Looting was hard work.

Jeff and Janet found the outer door to the animal pens to be unlocked. This was to be expected as no one regarded this part of the lab as high security. They emerged inside the small entrance way and were greeted by three doors.

"Which one of these doors do you want to take?" Jeff asked as he read the names of each of them. The signs were located in the center of each of the doors and read as follows: Reptile, Marine and Mammal.

"I can rule out door number one right now. I am not going near anything that might have snakes in it." Janet quickly said as she made sure to stay away from the first room.

"That leaves only one door because I sure as hell am not going in anything that could have sharks swimming around. Especially not zombie sharks. Fuck that." Jeff shot back as he started going for the third and final door marked mammals.

"Before we open this," Jeff said with his hand poised over the doorknob. "I want to make sure that they do not have lions or dogs or something big in there with large teeth."

"Not sure. I have never been in there." Janet admitted, but saw the look of trepidation on Jeff and added. "I am sure they would not let anything dangerous in here."

"You mean like a crazy scientist that creates zombies?" Jeff said sarcastically.

"OK, Fine." Janet conceded. "We will just have to go through the marine room to get there."

"Uh," Jeff paused staring at the small white sign affixed to the door to the marine room. "Suddenly this way isn't so bad."

Remaining ever cautious, he began listening at the door. He heard no barking or howling. He also heard nothing moving around so he slowly opened it. Ready to slam it shut at a moment's notice. The room smelled like an unkempt kennel. The stench assaulted them as they entered.

They could see the back door at the back of the large room from where they stood. However, they could also see overturned cages and the caretaker of the animal pens lying on the floor. The tables in the middle of the room were lined with metal trays that held syringes. Some still filled with whatever the scientists were injecting these poor animals with.

They stepped carefully towards the unmoving figure spread out on the floor. Making sure that they kept an eye out for any movement from her, no matter how slight it might seem to be.

They were within inches of the fallen woman when they suddenly heard a small sound coming from behind them. It sounded like something flopped onto the hard tile floor. Jeff watched the person lying on the floor while Janet chanced a look behind. She breathed a sigh of relief when she saw a small grey rabbit lazily staring at them.

"It's only a bunny." She sighed and mentally reminded herself that paranoia in this place is a good thing. "Should I call it over?"

"Just let it go." Jeff said never looking away from his target. "I would be more worried about getting out of here. Here's the plan. We are never going to know if that person is really dead or just waiting for us to get closer, unless we get closer. You have the gun, so I will check to see if it is a zombie."

Not bothering to wait for any protests that he knew would be coming, Jeff inched closer and closer making sure that it still had not moved. Finally, when he was within reach, he pushed out with his blade and nudged the woman's shoulder. No movement and no attack. All of these things Jeff took to be a good sign.

It seemed that he was not satisfied with his initial inspection because he then got even closer and proceeded to kick the poor lady hard enough to make her move.

"Well, if she didn't try to eat us after that, then I don't think she will." Jeff stepped over her and made his way to the door with Janet close behind.

"Isn't that cute?" Janet awed.

"What?" Jeff asked as he tried the door handle and cursed at it being locked.

"I think the little bunny likes us." She said and Jeff turned from his task to find that indeed the small grey rabbit had made a single hop towards them.

Jeff continued to stare as no less than four others had joined the first. What made him notice that something was not right was when the final bunny had slowly hopped from the shelf that must have held their cages. It seemed to be an odd color for a rabbit. Bright red streaked down one side. He looked at the other creatures to see if they had similar markings. That was when he noticed the truth.

When it had landed, and it took only a second for Jeff to realize what he was looking at when he stared into the red eyes and he heard the hissing coming from the chorus of tiny mouths.

"Oh shit." Jeff whispered and quickly went to work kicking at the locked door.

"What?" Janet yelled at his statement.

"Zombie fucking bunnies!" Jeff screamed as he kicked at the door repeatedly. Rattling the wooden frame with every shot.

As one the gathering of rabbits charged, still hissing that awful sound. Janet managed a few shots, yelling over the sounds, "They are too fast. Get that door open now!"

The nightmarish things were close enough that one more leap would send their sharp teeth sinking into the soft flesh of their waiting victims. With a final Herculean kick, the door flew open and nearly off of the hinges. Jeff and Janet scrambled through with her still firing shots behind them. She heard a small squeal as one of the rounds finally hit home.

Outside the animal pen was a small hall that held another door leading into Faustus' lab and if that one was locked, Jeff knew that they would not make it. He said a quick prayer that the door would be opened to them. *Death by fucking bunnies. I can just hear Chris laughing now.*

They raced up the hall as fast as possible with the little devils hot on their heels the entire way. Janet reached the door first and tried the handle. It opened and they rushed inside. She slammed the door with everything she had and you could hear the tiny bodies pounding against the door, unable to slow themselves down.

Jeff grabbed a small but sturdy cabinet and quickly slid it in front of the door.

"Jeff," Janet said calmly noticing his flushed face and his heavy breathing. "You know they can't open doors right?"

Panting, Jeff replied, "Not taking any chances."

They took their time in wandering around the lab, Janet saw the form of the late Dr. Faustus lying on the floor and she paused at the sight. Looking away from him, she saw the large pool of congealing blood next to one of the overturned gurneys and again she was thankful that she had not taken part in whatever had happened in here.

Jeff had seen Janet's reaction at the sight of the dead doctor. He walked over to one of the see through cupboards and took a blanket from inside. He then went and covered the man in order to spare Janet the image.

He looked at the large viewing window set beside the door of the lab and could not help but imagine the creatures standing outside as he saw the bloody handprints smearing the window. His resolve to leave this place grew and he set himself to looking for anything that could open the shutters.

A thorough search proved pointless as they found nothing that looked like a switch to open their cage. A defeated look crossed them both and Jeff said, "Let's just hope that Chris had better luck."

"So you want to know why you are still alive." Cheitan said with a casual air as if he were talking about the day's weather and not a man's life. "Let's just say that I have a need for you. I am sure that you have figured out that I am not, as you would say, from around here."

Cheitan paused although he expected no response from the cowering Alan Salvin. In truth he had hoped that the little man would not offer any kind of reply.

"It took a lot of planning and preparation for me to even be able to come here and quite a deal more for me to remain as long as I have. And that, my friend, is where you come in." Cheitan continued. He started to pace around the room, gathering his thoughts in an effort to best explain what was happening.

"You see, many millennia ago, before The Fall," Cheitan started. "The masters lived above, in paradise. I am sure you have heard this story Alan."

Alan nodded nervously. He knew what Cheitan was talking about. He had been a church going man at one time.

"Anyway, some of the masters had decided that they did not like the current management. They tried, and as you know, failed to take control from Him." Cheitan face took on a look of disgust as he kept on with his tale. "They were banished. Sent to live below in the deepest, darkest pits. They were never allowed to see their former home again. But did you know that was not the end of the story?"

Cheitan seemed to relish in not only the fear he was causing the shaking Alan, but it also appeared that he liked the sound of his own voice.

"After The Fall, He gave another decree. He gave us control over the Earth and all that was on it for a time. But there was a catch. We were never allowed to set foot on this plane. We could not touch anything here. We were only allowed the power of influence. We could whisper in your ear all manner of delectable sins, but only you could choose to do them. It is His way of testing you peasants. Seeing if you are worthy of Him."

That was when Cheitan stopped his pacing and glared directly into the eyes of the terrified Salvin. "And that is why I could not kill you. You see, I found a way around that little rule. I found a way to achieve physical form on this plane. I could do anything. Even kill. While it took me lifetimes, eventually I saw the path to my true freedom in the form of the late Dr. Faustus."

Marlin is dead? That was the only thought Alan's mind could form as his fear increased and his head filled with flashes of the ways he would undoubtedly be tortured to death.

"When he was fired from his last job, I found my, if you will forgive the expression, *salvation* in you. You and your greed that is." Cheitan moved even closer to

Alan, a slow laugh building inside of him. "You are the one I need to make my stay permanent. But first, I have to deal with a few pests that still roam these halls. Unfortunately, my plans are delicate and I must make sure that everything goes as planned. These little problems must be dealt with."

CHAPTER 11:

DESPERATION

Cheitan sat on the floor and seemed to retreat within himself. His eyes closed and his brow furrowed in deep concentration. Still, Alan Salvin did not dare make any kind of move towards the exit. Any movement would probably mean angering Cheitan and the thought of a pissed off Cheitan sent chills throughout Alan.

As he listened to the unbelievable story told by the large thing seated before him, Alan thought that he had begun to realize just what his part was in this grand scheme. If not for his hiring of Faustus, then there would have been no experiments. There would have been no deaths. At least not on his conscience anyway. This was his fault.

Cheitan began mumbling something in a language that Salvin had not heard before. He could barely make out the softly spoken words over the pounding of his own heartbeat.

Chetian focused every ounce of energy that he could spare into the task of searching the building, hoping to find the few remaining people that were still wandering its halls. Ever since the first time he sensed the presence of another attempting to enter his world, he had to make sure that his wards were stronger than ever. He would not abide someone interfering with his plans. This day must go off without a hitch.

With those thoughts in mind, he reached out to his wandering brothers. While they were not yet ready to accept his full command, they could understand the basic instructions he was about to give them.

He had sensed that the interlopers were wandering around the laboratory area. Focusing himself even harder, Cheitan saw that two of them were in the lab with what was left of Faustus and the other was in the doctor's room.

Seeing his opportunity, he sent a small suggestion to the creatures that he felt roving around in the holding area. They appeared to be just wandering aimlessly, unsure of anything other than what to eat next. Cheitan decided to give them something to eat. He gave them a small mental nudge to head out into the hall.

Now that the pesky business of dealing with the last survivors was over with, he brought himself out of his trance-like state and threw a dangerous stare at Alan Salvin.

"My brothers are on the hunt. They will take care of the pests still wandering in my building. Now, where were we? Ah yes, I was about to tell you why you still live."

All over the building, the undead roamed the halls with a single purpose. To consume whatever they felt was food. They shuffled through rooms and on the stairways aware of only the pain that they felt as they were devoured from the inside out. Confusion reigned as they searched for more prey for only the flesh of others could ease the agony that they felt.

Time and again that day the zombies had gorged themselves on the flesh and blood of the living; only to have those same victims join them in their Hellish nightmare of pain and hunger. The screams of their victims they could not understand. The pleading of the soon to be devoured fell on the deaf ears of the dead. There was no malice in their feeding. It was just what they did.

After a time, they found that the food no longer walked these halls. They could not smell the sweet, salty scent of the one thing that would dull the anguish of their existence. There were moments when peace seemed near only to be taken away again.

The time that the food was within reach, only to have it escape. Their moans increased in intensity, as they knew only that they had lost a brief respite from the suffering that filled their every cell.

Even worse for them was the time that they had laid hands on food only to have it taken from them. Some of them had tried to follow the food, but they were stopped. The food had gone. Unsure of what to do, they once again began wandering the halls. Some found themselves in an area that, had they the mental capacity for memories, they would find familiar.

The unmade beds and overturned chairs of the holding area drew no feelings of home or nostalgia from the creatures that now wandered these halls. Stumbling into the rooms without purpose, the zombies merely kept up their relentless pursuit for something to ease the hurting that dominated their unbearable reality.

Suddenly the group within the holding area shivered and convulsed. They still could feel the torment that seemed to be their life's purpose, but they felt something else as well. Something was telling them where food was. They could not explain how they knew nor would they even care to. As one the shambling horde began to make their way over fallen debris and out into the hallway where they were certain that something would come to them. Their moans reached a fevered level of intensity as they eagerly anticipated their next few minutes of pain free peace.

Chris sat on the edge of Faustus' bed as he finished his cold, refreshing Mountain Dew. *Never would have thought that a zombie-making psychopath would have such good taste in soda.* Chris thought as he drained the last of the can and threw it on the floor.

He ejected the clip from his pistol and went about removing the shells. He laid them out before him on the bed and counted only eight bullets remaining.

"At least I didn't have to meet with anything on my way here. Glad I didn't need that extra ammo that I gave Janet." Chris said more to hear something other than the prevailing silence he had been listening to for the last twenty minutes. He went about reloading the magazine, still surprised with himself that he knew so much about the weapon he picked up. He had never spent a day of his life at a firing range and the security company he had worked for never sent them for their proper training

Slamming the clip home into the gun and loading a bullet into the chamber, Chris made sure that he still had the journal he had found in the locked drawer. He picked it up and resigned himself to walking back to Jeff and Janet, hoping that they could get the shutters open and if not, that they could at least let him inside that lab.

Chris reached for the door, confident in his earlier sweep of the hall, and opened it. As he stepped out, he shut it a little harder than he would have liked, because when he looked up the hall he saw Hell coming for him.

There were only three of the undead lumbering in a straight line after him, but it was still three more that he had ever hoped to see outside of a movie. He looked over their shoulders and found that he could see the lab that still held Jeff and Janet within.

"I hope they see this. Janet will have to adjust her score-card." Chris said to the things slowly making their way to him. He threw off the safety and took careful aim.

Jeff found himself to be quite bored searching through the laboratory. He could not make heads or tails of anything he found. Strange chemicals and different sized containers lined each of the cabinets. Surprisingly, these sturdy pieces of glass and steel had not moved when the rest of the building had. Jeff had to assume that whatever was in there was pretty toxic and needed the extra precautions.

However, nothing that he had found had looked like a switch to open the steel shutters that still held them prisoner in this place that could be described as a nightmare, so their little run-in with the evil Easter Bunnies had so far not been worth the effort. He found that he could not concentrate on what he was doing so he turned back to the large window by the door. He was anxious to be looking anywhere but at more vials and papers.

Jeff looked over at Janet and saw that she was engrossed in a piece of paper that she had just pulled off of the floor. Admiring her ability to still remain professional and confident, even in the face of all of her co-workers trying to eat her, Jeff just stared for a few moments. Fearing that she would catch him staring at her, Jeff turned to look outside. That was when he saw what he was sure was a mirage. This could not be happening.

"Janet!" Jeff yelled and she was so startled that she dropped whatever she was looking at so intently only seconds before in order to run over to Jeff. "You need to see this."

"What is it?" She asked as she looked out the window, trying her best to ignore the streaked prints of blood partially blocking her view.

"Seems that we aren't the only ones that are having undead trouble." Jeff said a little to calmly as he saw the three creatures advancing on Chris. He also saw Chris raise his weapon so that he could reduce the number of fiends in the building.

Jeff cast a sidelong glance at Janet, unwilling to take his full attention away from Chris, and said, "I think he will be taking high score with this one."

Janet just stared at him and went to reply with a witty comment when she saw Jeff's face go white. She looked outside and saw the scene unfolding. Unwilling to believe it, she just kept telling herself that it was all part of some stupid plan that Chris had made up in order to impress them. She replayed the last few moments in her mind.

She saw Chris bring up the gun, that damn grin spread over his face as though he knew that she was watching. She noticed that he took careful aim for once. That was when it all went downhill quickly. She saw him try and pull the trigger. She saw him backing up as he looked at his gun, his only form of protection. His face showed both fear and confusion. Then she saw something she could not believe. He threw the gun at them.

Chris spared careful looks back at the window behind the things growing ever closer. Their pace was so slow that Chris knew that he had a minute to spare for his friends to watch him overcome these odds. Finally, he saw Jeff standing watch at the stained windowpane and knew that his audience had arrived.

Chris felt the surge of confidence that the pistol had bestowed upon him. He knew that he would be able to handle these undead things.

Bringing the sight of his pistol to rest on a dead white eye of the nearest zombie, Chris calmed himself and took a steadying breath. His aim would be perfect.

His shot would find its mark. These things he told himself as he squeezed the trigger, excitedly waiting for the loud crack of gunfire to echo off of the walls. None came. No sounds filled the hall except for the groaning of the dead creatures inching ever closer.

Chris looked at his gun and cursed loudly. It was jammed. One of the bullets had gotten stuck when the sliding mechanism of the gun tried to load it into the chamber.

Chris quickly tried to pry the shell out of the breach and found that it was impossible. A new feeling filled him then, dread. In a panic, he drew his hand back as far as he dared and launched the gun at his pursuers. The weapon bounced uselessly off of the chest of one of the creatures. They just kept on walking in their slow, unerring pace.

"You ain't got me yet!" Chris yelled at the zombies, who seemed oblivious to what was happening in the hall. Chris remembered the small office of Faustus and made for the door and relative safety. He reached out for the handle, ever aware that the creatures that he was so confident he could overtake were gaining on him with every second. He turned the knob. It was stuck fast.

"Dear God, just give me a fucking break!" Chris screamed as he threw his hands up to the Heavens. He slammed his shoulder into the door, hoping to rock it enough that it would open. It refused to budge. Now he had a sore shoulder and an advancing undead troupe to worry about.

Jeff screamed and cursed as he saw what was happening. He saw Chris try and make it back to

Faustus' room. He saw that he could not get in. Jeff went immediately to the door and tried to throw it open. The small keypad next to the door read *Locked.*

"We need to get the hell out there!" Jeff yelled and Janet jumped at the sudden outburst. "They're gonna kill him!"

"We can go through the animal pens again!" Janet suggested quickly and started for the back door.

"We can't!" Jeff said to stop her before she opened that door and let the tiny monstrosities inside the lab. "We go in there and Peter Zombietail will be all over us. There's just no time to kill them and get to Chris."

Jeff brought back a large, meaty fist and rammed it solidly against the pane of bloody glass. His shout of pain was the only thing he had accomplished. The glass would not break. He nearly sank to his knees as he realized that all he could do was watch as his best friend was devoured by the undead. Anger and frustration renewed him and he continued his pointless assault on the bulletproof glass. Another and still more bone shattering blows landed on the window and Jeff was screaming in pure rage at the barrier before him. The only thing that his efforts brought was more blood to add to the window. Thankfully, the streaks of the zombies' blood were on the other side.

Chris prepared himself for what he knew he must do. He would not simply lie down and let them have an easy time of feasting on his soft tissue. He noticed the drama being played out in the lab as Jeff tried to break the glass to reach him.

"No time for that buddy." Chris said getting ready for his foolish plan. He looked behind the walking dead and saw the side door that was between the first and last two zombies. "If I can reach that, I should be safe for a moment or two."

Chris knew that he was no star athlete. However, he would simply not accept the fact that his plan would fail. To do so would mean that he was dead already, and there were just too many things he had not yet done.

Drawing his legs beneath him, Chris prepared for a final sprint in what would surely be the stupidest thing he had ever done, and that is including a long list of idiotic dares he had accepted.

He studied the situation and had to force himself to not just run in a blind panic. Waiting for just the right moment when the door would be exactly between his tormentors, Chris readied himself for what might have been his final stand. Suddenly the time was right and he uncoiled his legs and took off with a sudden burst of speed.

`When he was close enough that he could see the dark red blood clotting on the face of the first creature and he could almost smell the rot on its breath, he leaped as high as he could. He thrust his foot out so that it would land squarely in the chest of the zombie. To attempt anything else would risk missing and having Chris land crotch first on the zombie's face. That was an experience Chris could live without.

His attack hit the mark perfectly. The undead thing fell backwards and landed solidly. Chris, with a good bit of momentum left in his leap, sailed over the fallen thing and landed just out of its reach. Maintaining his forward progress, Chris headed straight for the door that would mean either his salvation or his death.

Somewhere deep below the struggle happening for a man's life, Cheitan laughed and knew that his problems were over.

CHAPTER 12:

THE HUNT BEGINS

Chris reached for the doorknob praying that he would have better luck than his had been. Much to his relief, one of the large double doors swung open easily and he managed to slip inside. Before the door could close, a dry, rotten hand had forced itself into the crack. Eager to remove the obstruction before the rest of the creature could come through, Chris pulled on the door with every fiber of his being. A loud snap confirmed that the hand had broken off at the wrist. It landed on the floor, unmoving. Chris kicked it towards a darkened corner of the room, hoping to not have to look at it again.

Taking in he surroundings, Chris was rapidly searching for anything that was not currently among the living. The room appeared to be a wide-open area with no real place for anything to hide. Still a careful inspection would mean that he would not be attacked. That was always a good reason to be thorough in Chris' mind.

He checked under and around the large wooden desk that seemed to be the dominating piece of furniture in the room. He also took note of the large bank of monitors lining the wall beside the desk.

He took in each screen in turn and found that he could get a good view of nearly every part of the building. He saw that his recent attackers were still trying to get at him, as if the constant pounding that he heard as they battered the door was not an indication. He saw the other levels as well and made a careful note of just how many of the creatures he could see. The monitor that caught his attention however was the one that showed the inside of Faustus' lab.

On that one he could see Jeff and Janet walking around impatiently, animated gestures showed their elevated emotional state.

He decided to take a look at the desk in front of him and found a few things that he thought were interesting. The first thing that he found was a daily planner, the kind that executives used to map out every second of their day. What was most interesting about it was the name of the person using it, Alan Salvin.

"So this is what the office of the big boss looks like. Not really that impressed." Chris said to himself. "I wonder what other goodies I can find in here."

He continued to browse the contents of the desk and as he moved aside a large stack of books that had fallen over, he found a small intercom. Pressing the button, Chris said, "Hello."

Jeff had managed to calm himself down. Having seen the results of Chris' foolhardy plan actually succeed, Jeff set himself to the task of trying to find a way out of the room. He was talking to Janet and each of them were giving ideas that seemed as unlikely as the next, when suddenly he just stopped talking. A look of bewildered shock crossed his face as he listened harder for something he was sure was all in his head. There it was again. Coming from the small speaker box next to the doorway, they distinctly heard Chris say, "Hello."

Janet was the first to reach the intercom and punched the call button. "Chris, is that you?" She asked still not sure if this was real or not.

Chris' voice came back through the static filled speaker, "Yep. Hey you see those moves?" His bravado hid the reality that he was amazed he had made it inside the room alive.

This time it was Jeff who would answer, "What moves? My Grandma has better moves." His relief could be heard by Chris at the other end of the connection. "Listen, we need to get out of here. Think you can find a way to open this door?"

A few moments' pause as Chris looked around for anything that might open the laboratory. "I have to look around. Don't go anywhere."

"Couldn't if we wanted to." Jeff replied sarcastically.

Chris went back to searching the room looking for anything that looked like a switch. He had only the small desk lamp and the soft glow from the monitors to work with, but it seemed as if someone was smiling upon him because he saw something that looked out of the ordinary. Along the one wall there was a panel of wood that just did not seem to fit properly.

Chris reached for the panel and pulled it aside, where it fell off of its hinges to land on the floor with a loud thud. Inside was a sight that made Chris squeal with glee. It was the controls for the gates. He reached for the first set of switches and realized that they had a small covering of Plexiglas and he was unable to reach them.

The computer screen embedded into the back of the wall came to life and on it was a single word and a flashing cursor. That word was "Password."

Chris cursed and stared at the blinking cursor for a few more seconds before he went back and told Jeff what he had just found. Jeff was just as disappointed as Chris was and Janet could be heard screaming curses at the deceased doctor.

"Well did you at least find a way out of here for us?" Jeff asked hopefully.

In truth, the finding of the gate controls had thrust his first mission out of his mind. His excitement at having found a way to open the building had overtaken everything else. "Not yet." Chris said and he heard the frustration coming from Jeff as he asked Chris to keep looking.

"By the way." Chris said suddenly as he remembered the journal he had retrieved from Faustus' office. "Tell Janet I found this notebook in that Faustus guy's room. Has all kinds of calculations and experiments in it. I had to break a locked drawer to get it."

"So." Jeff said back, placing one hand to his forehead trying to soothe the headache that was sure to come from this conversation. "You found a notebook in a locked drawer." He paused hoping that Chris would be able to follow where his train of thought was going.

'Yep." Chris said and Jeff heard the obviously proud tone in his voice.

OK Chris. Don't make me have to tell you what should be coming next. Jeff thought to himself as he did not hear anything else from Chris.

"So you found it in Faustus' office huh?" Jeff asked again, trying to give him one more try. Dead air was all that answered him. "Have you thought of looking in there for the password to this damn door?"

"Hey!" Chris said cheerfully. "That is a great idea. Let me take a look and I will get back to you."

Jeff started pounding his head against the door, amazed at how Chris could seem so intelligent one minute and a complete moron the next. And just as he predicted, here came that headache.

A short time later, Chris' voice could be heard over the intercom again and he said, "Ready guys? I was looking in here and the password was listed right on the front cover. It's 9-4-8-7-1. Hurry up and get over here."

Jeff let him know that he received it. He turned to Janet who had been listening intently the entire time.

"You ready to get out of here?" Janet asked as she went to the keypad. She checked her gun and they made a final glance out of the window, seeing that the three undead still lurked outside the office where Chris was.

"Looks like you have to save his ass." Jeff said to Janet. "Try not to rub it in too much though."

Janet smiled and said, "I make no promises."

With that Janet entered the code and Jeff held the door open just enough so that they could target the creatures attacking the door. She fired off a single round that found its mark. The zombie dropped quickly as the remains of its skull scattered across the others. As one they turned and started to make their way towards the lab.

Careful aim had allowed Janet to subdue the final two undead and clear the way to get to Chris and the way out. Before they even reached the room, Chris opened the doors for them, making sure that he slammed the doors into as many of the truly dead creatures as he could.

"Welcome to my home." Chris said with a deep bow as Janet and Jeff pushed past him.

Jeff paused, looked at Chris and said, "Dork."

"Yeah, yeah." Chris said as he waved the comment away. He turned and followed them into the room. "So what have you guys been up to while I was almost eaten?"

Cheitan sat in his sanctuary, mentally keeping track of how is brothers were faring. He had sensed them trap one of the guards. Cheitan also felt the delicious fear, as the fool knew he was trapped. The next thing he knew, Cheitan felt the wailing moans of the ones he had sent on the hunt as their quarry escaped.

Frustrated, Cheitan threw Alan Salvin forcefully from the small chair he had been resting on and proceeded to smash it against the nearest wall. He returned to the center of the protective circle on the floor and made a decision. He was losing too many of his family. He had to move his plans up. The time to remake the world was here.

"Mr. Salvin. It is soon time for you to play your true role in this little game." Cheitan laughed maniacally as he looked into the eyes of his captive.

Chris had his head on the desk. Overcome with emotion, tears flowed rapidly from his eyes. He pounded his fist on the desk in an effort to regain control of himself. He threw his head back, trying to take in a breath that did not want to come. Finally sweet oxygen entered his lungs and the raucous sound of laughter could be heard echoing throughout the room.

In between sharp intakes of breath, Chris said, "Should have had Elmer Fudd with you!" He looked up to see the serious faces of Jeff and Janet and this just set him to laughing harder.

As one, Jeff and Janet made noises of disgust and anger. Janet looked at him furiously and said, "To think we were worried about you." She turned and walked to the monitors.

"Oh, come on guys." Chris pleaded. "If it was me that had the bunnies, you know you would be laughing. Besides, everyone made it out fine. I mean, everyone except for the dead guys outside the door."

Janet was further infuriated by the lack of respect Chris was showing to her diseased and deceased coworkers. Jeff just continued to stare at him, unable to make up his mind if he was truly mad. Because if the truth were to be told, Jeff would have been laughing if it didn't happen to him.

Chris decided that discretion was the better part of valor and began apologizing to Janet. After many minutes of this, Jeff said finally, "Look. What we need to do now is find a way to get those damn gates open. Then we can argue about what an insensitive ass Chris is."

They all nodded in agreement and began looking around the room. Chris handed Janet the notebook and day planner he had found. She sat in the leather office chair and began pouring over the notes.

Suddenly, Janet tells the guys to come over so that they can take a look at the notes. Chris and Jeff lean in, but quickly step back as they realize that, while the language is English, they cannot understand a word of what is written.

"Um, Janet dear." Jeff began carefully, painfully remembering her past outbursts. "We can't read geek, I mean scientist." Jeff added quickly as he noted the look in Janet's eyes. Chris had seen it as well and had since learned to just step back and wait for the fireworks.

When none came, Chris chanced a few cautious steps back to the desk. A sudden thought dawned on him. He looked at Jeff and said, "Did you just call her *dear*?"

Jeff went pure scarlet as he stumbled over himself in an effort to explain without letting Janet know how he truly felt. Inane babbling poured from Jeff as he fought to regain control.

As Chris retreated to the far side of the room in order to hide another fit of laughter, Janet simply looked at Jeff and smiled. "I didn't mind." She whispered to him.

All of a sudden, Jeff forgot that he was locked in a crumbling building surrounded by the undead each wanting a piece of him to chew on. A broad smile was evident on his face and he said, "Actually Janet. There was something…"

His speech was cut short as Janet jumped out of her seat and walked quickly to the monitors. The one that showed the outside of their room held something they had definitely not expected. There was someone waving at them.

They stared for what seemed like ages at the monitor. Surely they could not be seeing what was being shown to them. One of the creatures that Janet had just destroyed was sitting where it had fallen with its back against the far wall, away from the doors. The strange part was that it was waving at them.

Chris started to tell Janet that she needed to work on her aim, when she was seen walking towards the door. They could clearly see that the hall was empty except for the waving zombie. The guys followed her more out of morbid curiosity than anything else.

Janet fired another round into the skull of the waver and still it just kept up its strange behavior. She was growing more and more frustrated. She took more careful aim, telling herself that she had just missed, when Jeff told her to stop.

Confused, she turned to look at him and before he could say anything, he put a finger to his lips to let her know to be quiet. There it was again. Faintly, he heard something coming from the creature. Were they really words?

Thankfully the waving had stopped and Jeff dared to take a few steps closer. He knelt down in front of the thing, unsure of why he did that and he clearly heard it say softly, "We need to talk."

CHAPTER 13:

THE LIST

Ascaroth knew that he had little time left to complete his tasks. Cheitan was gathering strength by the second and he would soon be ready to finish what he started. Ascaroth had no choice, he had to find a way to slow him down. There was one who might be able to help him.

Ascaroth made his way down the darkened paths that would lead him to the Dark Library, and most importantly, to the means to at least stall Cheitan.

The Dark Library was one of the most famous buildings in their realm. It stood taller than any other and contained every book ever written. Shelves held aged tomes and newer materials as well. Books were piled all along halls where there was simply no more room to hold them all. He entered the aged structure and was instantly met by its caretaker.

"Hello again Ronwe." Ascaroth said greeting the aged figure before him. "It has been too long."

"Yes it has." Ronwe went over to greet Ascaroth, leaning heavily on an old walking stick that had seen better days. "Not that I do not appreciate the visit, but what brings you here?"

"I thought for certain that the keeper of knowledge would know what was going on around him.' Ascaroth said as he grinned at his friend.

"Of course I know." Ronwe said laughing along with Ascaroth. "I have all of the books you need in the room over there." Ronwe gestured towards a small alcove set off to one side of the large entrance hall.

Ascaroth said his thanks and went to begin his research. Pouring over the words with a speed that was fueled by the urgency of the task at hand. The longer he took to find what he needed, the father along Cheitan would be. His only hope was that Cheitan felt safe with his barrier in place and did not feel the need to hurry.

After going through many of the ancient books, Ascaroth finally happened upon something that might help. He picked up the book and turned to leave when a large hand landed on his shoulder.

"Can't let you have that." A deep voice said.

Ascaroth sighed. To say that he did not expect some resistance would be incorrect. He knew that the followers of Cheitan would try to stop him, but he had expected better. To send this one was almost in insult.

"Hello Acham." Ascaroth sighed. "Please don't tell me that you are the one sent to stop me."

"I will stop you. Our time to rise draws near and there is no one who will stop us." Acham said proudly as he reached for the book held in Ascaroth's hand.

"Acham, you are the Demon of Thursday." Ascaroth said smiling. "Really, does it get more pathetic?"

"He is not alone." Came another voice from the darkened corner.

Ascaroth shuddered slightly. "Ah, Byleth. I had heard that you joined the upstart. I was hoping that I had heard wrong. I am here on direct orders from the master. To impede me would be to defy him."

Any hope that Ascaroth had carried that they would leave him alone based solely upon learning who had sent him quickly was dashed. An angry gleam flashed in their eyes as they advanced on him, slowly stalking him. Ascaroth was no stranger to battle. He had been in more than one, but Byleth was one of the kings. He knew the power Byleth possessed.

Immediately Ascaroth sought out the weaker of his opponents, hoping to at least make the number of fighters even. His small stature made it both harder for him to reach his attackers, but also harder for them to hit him. He dodged a large overhand blow that only connected with the hard stone table behind him. Ascaroth ducked under and came up with a leaping grab at the throat of Acham, tearing at the soft tissue of his neck. Acham's eyes went wide as he felt the muscles in his neck separate from him. Blood poured freely from the wound and just as quickly Ascaroth circled around behind Acham to watch him struggle and fall.

Byleth stood by watching the display, waiting for his time to strike. As Ascaroth had his attention focused on the falling Acham, Byleth shot a hard kick into the side of Ascaroth's head. Ascaroth flew through the air to land amidst a stack of books older than the recorded history of men. Sending them falling in all directions.

Byleth, remaining confident and calm, walked over to Ascaroth and pulled him to his feet. "The *master* does not rule us any longer. We will have our own realm." A backhand sent Ascaroth into another stack of books, decimating the precious volumes.

Ascaroth, vision blurred, did not see the next attack coming. He did, however, feel the booted heel slam into the side of his head. He felt his skull nearly crack under the onslaught. Ascaroth waited for the next blow that would surely finish him, but a sudden wisp of smoke assailed his nostrils and he knew that no other attack would come.

His eyes swollen, Ascaroth could only listen to the screams and tearing of flesh and the one time king was now a thing of history. Byleth was gone.

"Get up." The voice of his master ordered.

"Thank you sire." Ascaroth said as he forced himself to his feet.

"That was not done for you. I cannot stand idly by and let one of my highest-ranking generals betrays me." The voice reached a new low as Ascaroth's master leaned in close and said, "You would do well to remember this."

The voice grew slightly more relaxed as it said, "Did you find what you need here?"

"Yes my master." Ascaroth said proudly.

The malice returned as he said, "And yet here you are, wasting time. Why are you not using this knowledge?"

"I go immediately sire."

The last thing he heard as he left the Dark Library was the master's voice telling Ronwe to place the heads of each of the traitors on poles and display them outside.

Ascaroth reached the clearing once again and reached out to sense where the ones who could help him were located. He found them much more quickly, which meant that Cheitan was diverting more of his attentions elsewhere. The only thing that could distract him now, was if he was preparing the final stages.

An urgency filled Ascaroth as he wondered how to best communicate with them. Then he saw his way.

Jeff jumped nearly out of his skin as when he heard the bullet-riddled corpse speak. "Didn't know they could do that." He said as he stepped back to stand beside Janet and Chris.

"Not supposed to." Chris added, still stunned at their discovery. "Should we shoot it again?" Chris looked at his fallen gun and longed for the feeling it gave him.

"Helped before." Came the soft whisper from the mouth of the undead as rotten air was expelled from decaying lungs.

"Wait a minute." Chris said holding his hands before him. "Are you saying that you are the thing from the lab before? The bubble writer?"

"Yes." Again his voice was barely more than a whisper.

"And you still think that this thing is not evil?" Chris said as he gestured at the possessed zombie.

Jeff ignored any comments he was about to make. They had to leave this place and fast. Any help was better than none. "We have to trust it. Do you know how to get out of here?" Chris shook his head no and resigned himself to being forced to listening to the creature's advice.

"OK then zombie whisperer." Chris said. "Have at it then. I, on the other hand, will be over there." Chris walked back inside the office.

"Good idea." The voice said. "Inside."

"No fucking way." This time it was Janet's turn to protest. "Sorry, but I will not be helping to drag that thing anywhere."

"Fine." Jeff said upset that his best friend and the girl of his dreams were both being insane. Really, so they had to drag a zombie into the room so that it could tell them what to do next. What could be the harm in that? Jeff thought all of those things and more as he pulled the legs of the creature, eager to stay away from the mouth, and brought it into the office.

"Have a new friend do you?" Chris said from behind the desk.

"Get out of that chair." Jeff said as he drug the zombie towards the desk, straining from the exertion. "I am sick of bending over. I want you to help me put him in the chair."

"I would rather shave my testicles with a cheese grater." Chris said in a tone that meant he would not change his mind.

"Stop being a sissy and help me." Jeff yelled. Chris begrudgingly got out of his chair and went to stand on one side of the talking dead. They started to lift him into the chair when suddenly; the thing fell out of Chris' grip.

Chris screamed and dropped the arm that had come off of the zombie. He proceeded to brush himself off with any scrap of paper he could find. It was Jeff's turn to laugh.

Jeff managed to get the body into the chair even without the help. When he finished, Janet reluctantly came over so that she could at least hear what was being said.

The story that they were told was done in broken sentences and Janet was taking notes on a small tablet she had found on the desk.

"Need to stop him." The voice said. "In basement." The rancid stench given off each time it spoke caused them to step a little father back. "Bind him."

The voice went on for a few more minutes telling them what they needed to do in order to accomplish this new task set before them.

Janet studied the list before her. The items seemed simple enough to get; salt, a mirror, a sharp knife, rope, some kind of small bowl and some candles. Most of these could be found lying around. The search should not take too long.

"Let me see if I got this straight. Someone, who is currently living in the basement of this place, made these zombies on purpose. He used Faustus to help him get it done. Now to stop him, we need to get his freaky ass away from the basement and BIND HIM, which I still can't believe I am saying, to somewhere farther away. Right?" Janet summarized the notes she had written.

She started to set her tablet on top of the desk, when the voice said, through decaying vocal cords, " Yes." A deep breath was seen being taken as the rotted chest rose and fell. It spoke in the barely audible whisper that they had grown accustomed to and said, "One more thing."

"Not a chance in hell." Chris said as they finished listening to the final words that came from the dead creature seated in the chair before them.

"Chris," Jeff said sympathizing with his friend. "I am not looking forward to this either, but we have to put an end to these things and if this is how we have to do it, then it must be done."

"I know, I know." Chris said reluctantly resigning himself to doing the unthinkable, now fully understanding the need for rope.

"Alright guys." Janet said as she finished studying the list. "We can get the knife from Faustus' lab. I saw a few scalpels in there. That should be good enough. The rest is on the floor above us. Cafeteria will have the salt we need and the supply closet upstairs has candles from a birthday party we had last month. No idea where to get the bowl though."

"Not a problem." Jeff said. "I packed my lunch today. I have one in there."

"Very good guys." Chris said impatiently as he ushered them outside and on their way to finally escaping. "Let's just get to the lab and get this over with. We still have to get these things to an office far away from the basement. I say we use Levine's. Would serve him right. Can't we just use our own blood though? Do we have to get one of them?"

"You heard him," Jeff sighed, just as unwilling to retrieve the last item on the list. "The blood must come from one of them. The voice said that since he made them, they are connected to him."

This time it was Janet's turn to make her apprehensions known. "So just how are we going to get one of these zombies up a few flights of stairs anyway?"

"No idea." Chris and Jeff said in unison and they reached for the door to Faustus' laboratory.

CHAPTER 14:

BEST LAID PLANS

As they sat inside Faustus' lab, carefully planning how to best get upstairs, each coming up with plans that they had hoped would not involve more encounters with the undead. "Alright." Janet said as she wrote each plan on the whiteboard she had picked up from the floor with a marker she pulled from under a cabinet. "We know we can use the elevators, so that should be our first stop."

"I still have to ask," Jeff said sitting cross-legged on the floor and raising his hand as though this were still high school. "What if when those doors open, a bunch of zombies are waiting to get on?"

"That would definitely rate high on the this-sucks-ometer.' Chris agreed nodding as he perched on the only clean lab table that still remained upright.

"Here is what we do." Janet offered, excited for her plan. "We go back to the office, look at the monitors, and if we see anything on that level near the elevator, we take the stairs. Sound like a plan?"

The guys approved of the idea and went to check the monitors inside Salvin's office. Finding the immediate area around the elevator zombie free, they decided that it was the safest and fastest way to get upstairs. They pushed the call button for the elevator and waited as the elevator lowered itself to their level, creating enough noise to make the group nervous.

"Must you complain about everything?" Jeff asked as he turned to look behind himself at Chris. "Duck!" Jeff screamed and grabbed Chris to force him out of the way of the thing sneaking up behind him, unheard, thanks to the racket of the descending elevator.

Janet brought her gun up to fire, but quickly saw that there was no need. Jeff had already buried the edge of his blade into the monster's skull, dropping it immediately to the floor. Jeff wrenched his blade out of the skull of the creature and turned to see if the elevator had arrived. He saw the look of shock on Janet's face and was about to say something both comforting and witty when she did something he had not been expecting. Another of the shambling masses had showed itself from around the corner of the hall leading to the waiting area for laboratory technicians.

"Sammy?" Janet said suddenly. Sorrow spread throughout her as she recalled her narrow escape. It seemed like a lifetime ago. Tears welled within her eyes as she stared into the cloudy, white eyes of the approaching monster. "I am so sorry. I should have come back when you called for help. It is my fault you got hurt." With resolve set strongly upon her face, she brought her gun up and said, "At least I can make it right." And she fired on her former friend, ending the torment that she was sure he was living in.

Just then the elevator arrived and they stepped on, pressing the button for the second floor.

"Gotta ask guys." Chris said as the doors closed. "If the sound of this thing drew those two, do you think there might be one or two waiting outside when we get up there?"

"Now you mention this." Janet said angrily. "After we are already on the way?" She sighed again in frustration, unable to do anything about the elevator's ascent and the potential fight they would have.

The extremely short ride only added to the tension building up within the small confines of the elevator. Jeff stood at the ready with his blade and Janet raised her pistol. The door opened and a loud crack echoed off of the walls.

"Jumpy much?" Chris asked grinning and staring at the small wisp of smoke coming from the end of Janet's gun.

"I hate you." Janet said as she walked out of the lift and into the zombie free hall.

They walked into the cafeteria to retrieve the salt. Moaning could be heard echoing off of the tile walls and in the far corner of the room they spotted a lone zombie lurking around the vending machines. A single shot sent the undead sprawling into the closest machine and landing on top of the spilled food.

"Damn." Jeff said. "Some of that might have been good yet." He looked at the wasted morsels with sadness in his eyes.

"I know." Chris said soothingly and then cast a pitying glare at Janet. "She just didn't know any better. Have to forgive her this once."

Jeff nodded and turned to look at Janet. "It's alright. We forgive you."

Janet stormed past both of them yelling, "You are both extreme dorks." She grabbed handfuls of salt packets and began stuffing them into her pockets. She turned to tell them more of what she thought when she spotted the saltshakers sitting on the tables. She added these to her already growing supply and readied herself for getting the next item on the list.

As they left the cafeteria, the guys stole a final look at the ruin that had encompassed the once fine eating establishment. A small sigh escaped them as they turned to head for the supply closet. Janet shook her head disapprovingly and walked on without a word.

After getting the candles, they started back towards the elevator. Chris tapped Janet on the shoulder. "I need to borrow the gun for a few minutes."

"For what?" She asked, casting him a puzzled look.

Chris looked around nervously, 'I have to use the bathroom."

"It's not that big." Jeff said laughing.

Janet barely stifled her own laugh as she handed Chris the gun.

"It's in case there is anyone else in there." Chris said as he reached for the handle to the men's room. "Getting eaten is one thing. Getting eaten while on the crapper is another."

"We are in a building full of zombies and you decide to take a bathroom break." Jeff said in disbelief. Chris simply shrugged and walked inside the restroom, taking care to listen and watch for potential dangers.

Finding the immediate area clear, Chris went about checking the stalls for undead feet. The precaution turned out to be a wise decision because when he reached the third stall, he noticed a pair of loafers underneath the door.

Chris prepared himself for a quick kill as he turned the small handle on the stall door. The creature inside burst out, arms stretched out before him reaching for Chris.

Chris backed up quickly, all thoughts of actually using the restroom for its intended purpose forgotten. He raised the gun and pulled the trigger. A sickening click was all that he heard. The gun was empty.

He turned and ran outside as fast as possible. Jeff and Janet still waited patiently for him. Seeing his state of panic, Jeff said, "Not go as planned huh?"

Chris thrust the gun at Janet, "Empty."

They understood then the hasty exit Chris had made.

"Want me to go in there and take care of it for you?" Jeff asked as Janet put the other clip into the pistol.

"No thanks. I think I can hold it." With those final words, they went to the elevator to make their way to the first floor. The elevator's slow ascension did not ease their feeling of dread for the coming events.

The elevator doors opened on a scene they had not expected. A hand reached in to grab at any source of living flesh it could get a hold upon. The mournful wailing that the other creatures they had encountered reached a new level as a hand fell on Janet's arm, jerking her towards it's eager mouth and causing her to drop her gun.

The zombie held on to her and started to pull her close enough to be within reach of its hungry jaws.

Janet was screaming for help and Chris and Jeff grabbed the creature trying to pry its hand from her. Panic and surprise had overtaken the group as they each took in the events. The zombie's mouth came close enough that Chris could feel the breath on his neck. Then just as suddenly, it was gone and the creature stopped that terrifying moaning and silence seemed to fill the lobby.

Jeff was the first to speak. "Everyone OK?"

Janet was shaken up by the experience and Chris just looked at the headless body lying on the floor. He looked at Jeff and a sudden realization dawned upon him. "You killed it. Not that I am not grateful, because I was almost eaten, but don't you think it was a bit close to my head when you did that?"

"A chance I was willing to take." Jeff said as he looked at his handiwork. "Turned out fine if you ask me."

Chris leaned in closer to Jeff and asked in a quiet voice, "Think she's gonna snap again?"

Chris felt a sharp blow to the back of his head and saw stars. Trying to clear his vision, he heard Janet say angrily, "*She* is fine. Let's just hurry up and get this over with." She bent down and retrieved her fallen weapon.

"Right." Jeff agreed quickly. "I'll just go over and get my lunch."

Chris reached down and grabbed one of the fallen inspirational posters that still had most of the frame intact. He brought it over his head and was about to plant the peppy saying right behind Janet's ears when he dropped it suddenly and said, "Damn."

The others turned to look at him and glanced suspiciously at the fallen poster. Chris hurried to continue, eager to turn their attention away from his abandoned attempt at assault, "You remember earlier with Fat Mike and you walking in with the game system?"

A small whimper came from Jeff at the painful reminder of the ruined videogame. "Yeah. What about it?"

Chris went on, "Did you have your lunch with you then?"

A look of shock came over Jeff, as he replied, "No I left it in the car."

Janet looked upset, which seemed to happen more often lately, but Chris had one final hope. "Did you get it while I was on rounds?"

Jeff thought back to that moment before all of this horror. "Let's see. I was playing the game. Corning called and I told him you wanted his job." At this Chris just stared at the pure evil that was his friend. "Janet came in and then you came downstairs all jealous that Levine was mounting your woman. Then we got called down to Corning's office and you know the rest."

Chris raised a hand to slap the smirk off of Jeff's face. Janet stepped in and said, "So what you are telling me is that there is no bowl."

"Pretty much." Jeff answered.

Janet just grumbled under her breath and walked over to the main desk of the lobby. When she had calmed down, she walked back and said, "Fine. There has to be something we can use as a bowl around here. Just look around."

"Does it have to be a small bowl or can it be a big bowl?" Chris asked.

"I don't care if it is the fucking Super Bowl, just find one!" She yelled and turned away.

"What is your problem?" Chris said angrily as he grabbed hold of Janet's arm.

Janet wheeled around to face him and said, practically screaming, "I am sick of you! I am sick of the way you make idiotic jokes constantly! My friends are downstairs right now. All of them are dead and some of them, in case you failed to notice, have just tried to eat me! Yet all you can do is make jokes."

Shocked, for once Chris was at a loss for words. He turned to look at Jeff, hoping for some kind of support. Jeff threw his hands in the air making it clear that he wanted no part of this.

"Listen." Chris said calmly, trying to diffuse the situation.

"No you listen." Janet yelled as she turned and thrust a finger at Chris' chest. "What is it you have done here besides having to get rescued by us?"

"I've done a lot of things." Chris said defensively. "I found the way out."

"You mean the one we can't use?"

Chris stuttered his next words as again he looked to Jeff for help. "Jeff. Tell her all of the things I did."

Jeff started to say something, but she cut him off before a single word could escape his lips. "Don't go looking for him to defend you. If you can't remember a single thing you did, at least make something up!"

"Just relax." This time it was Jeff that stepped in and started walking over to intervene and stop the fight. "This is not going to get us out of here any faster."

"Neither will saving his ass every ten minutes!" Janet yelled back.

"Jeff, calm down your old lady. She is about a second away..." Chris was interrupted again by the shrill voice of Janet.

"Old lady?" She turned to plead with Jeff. "See what I mean? He can't go a few seconds without a smart remark."

"Look, that is just how he deals with things." Jeff tried to explain.

"Yeah," Chris said, anger filling him. "We can't all go catatonic and huddle in a corner."

Janet huffed and she raised her right hand to point at Chris. That was the hand that held the gun. Chris dove out of the way and Jeff stepped in front of her. She looked down and saw what she was doing and quickly lowered her hand.

Chris picked himself off of the floor and looked at Janet as though she had just become one of the zombies. "Dude, your chick is psycho. We need to get out of here and she just tried to shoot me. Calm her down or tie her ass up until we get out of here."

Jeff stared at the floor, wanting nothing more than for this argument to have never happened. He slowly picked up his head and asked, "Could you maybe tone down the kidding a bit? I know how you mean it, but she doesn't know you that well yet."

"You are taking her side?" Chris gasped, unable to believe what he was hearing.

"I'm not taking…" Jeff started to explain but was cut off again.

"Fine. Maybe I will take my useless ass back downstairs and find a way out of here. Alone." Chris turned and walked back to the elevator, kicking the head of their most recent encounter out of his way.

"Now maybe we will get something done!" Janet yelled after him.

Jeff shot her a look and started to go after his friend to get him to stay.

Chris stood inside the elevator. As he hit the door close button, he leaned around and gave the middle finger to Janet.

Chapter 15:

Most Dangerous Game

Jeff and Janet entered one of the many offices they had been searching, each starting to resemble the other. A soft glow from the emergency lighting was the only source of illumination. These rooms were in much the same shape as the rest of the building.

An eerie silence filled the room that had nothing to do with the death that surrounded them. Neither of them had said anything to each other as they looked for the next item on their list.

As they looked around the familiar looking area, Janet said, "Sorry about that back there. Everything just exploded."

Jeff stopped what he was doing, turned to look at her in the dimly lit room and said, "Not me you should be apologizing to."

"I know." She said as she looked down at her hands. "I think the best thing we can do now though is to finish this list and get those doors open. We can talk about the rest later."

"Sure." Jeff said, feeling nervous for what he was about to do. "Maybe we can talk about it over dinner or a movie."

Janet, realization suddenly dawning on her about what was happening, said, "Are you asking me out?" She grinned at the shade of red that Jeff had turned.

"Yeah...kinda..." Jeff stammered. He mentally kicked himself for saying that. He had wanted to ask her out for quite a long time now, but why had he picked this moment? *What if she says no. Can't play it as a joke. Especially with how she just went off about that kind of thing.* Jeff thought this and many other things as he busied himself with looking around the room, all thought of what he was searching for so reverently forgotten.

He was so intent on his own thoughts that he never heard Janet speaking. She had to throw a stapler at him to get his attention.

"For the third time," Janet said exasperated. "I would love to go."

Relief flooded Jeff and he found he could finally concentrate on the task at hand.

He looked puzzled for a moment before he said, "Why does it have to be a bowl? Can't we just grab one of these potted plants and take one of the pots?"

"You may just be on to something." Janet said smiling at more than just his suggestion. They looked around and quickly found a small round vase with floating candles suspended on tiny plastic leaves.

Jeff turned the entire contents over onto the floor. Janet gave him a disapproving look and he said, "I think the company will have worse things to worry about than a wet office rug." He tucked the bowl underneath his arm and went to check the list.

They now only needed a mirror, a length of rope and an undead sacrifice.

Chris slammed the stop button on the elevator halfway between floors one and two. "Useless huh? I show her fucking useless." He ranted and yelled to himself for another few minutes before a sudden idea filled his overzealous mind.

He hit the start button and let the elevator continue down to the third floor, which he now realized could have an undead horde waiting for him. The elevator came to a sudden stop and the doors dinged open. Outside stood a lone creature. It turned to face him and started walking faster now that it had his scent.

As Chris slammed a hand onto the door close button, he quickly formed a plan. The creature was mere feet away before the door started closing and by the time it finished, the hand was scraping the door.

Chris' plan could be called foolhardy by some and completely idiotic by the rest. *All I have to do is get the rope from the flag poles in the lobby and then we will see who is the worthless one. Once I bring him up here I will shove it right in her face. Maybe literally.*

Chris' grin had no humor in it as he thought of Janet screaming when the creature grabbed onto her. *Where would she be if we hadn't helped her scrawny ass? Just another dead thing walking around this place, that's where.*

Chris stepped out of the elevator and into the lobby. He heard movement upstairs and saw the two of them walking around. *Probably still looking for that damn bowl.*

Chris ran over to the flagpoles that stood beside the main doors and proceeded to remove the lengths of rope from both poles. He then tied them together and made a noose around one end. As an added precaution, he took the smaller of the flagpoles and broke it in half.

Sparing glances at the upper floors to see where Jeff and Janet were, Chris went back to the elevator, determined to make them see his worth.

A sudden thought struck him like a thunderbolt, would it really be the most intelligent of ideas if he were to stand inside an elevator with one of those things? Deciding that it would not be a great idea, Chris went for one of the spare chairs kept in the lobby for guests waiting for someone to call them to their office.

He dragged the chair back to the elevator and once inside he stood on it to ease his way through the service hatch above. He then reached down and pushed the button for the third floor with the long pole he took from the lobby. Now all he had to do was wait and once the doors opened, that one zombie would walk inside. All he would have to do is slip the noose around its neck and then use the pole to hit the first floor button.

Sure dragging the thing upstairs once he go out of the elevator would be difficult, but he would deal with that little hitch in his plan when he got to that point. He wanted to see if the rest of his plan worked before worrying about the rest of it.

He waited nervously as the elevator made its noisy descent, hoping and dreading the next phase of his plan. He slid the length of rope down through the hole, making the opening wide enough so that he could easily grab the creature. The doors opened when he reached his destination and he waited patiently for the thing to saunter into the small space. A few times he had to hit the door open button.

His patience was wearing thin and his adrenaline rush was beginning to wear off. Chris now wondered if the thing was still waiting outside or if it had left to search the halls once more.

Chris leaned down into the elevator car and tried his best to look out through the door. He had to catch himself from falling the first time, but after readjusting his position, he saw that the hall was empty.

"Now where the hell did he run off to? The first time I want a zombie around and I can't find one." Chris said as he scanned the hall from the safety of his perch. Noting the lack of undead, Chris lowered himself to the floor and resigned himself to going on the hunt for one of them.

As he stepped out of the elevator, the doors began to shut.

"Can't let that happen." Chris said as he placed his makeshift stool between the doors to hold them open. As he neared the first intersection, which led to the supply closet, he chanced a look back to see if the doors were still open. Sure enough, the doors would attempt to close, only to bang against the stool and then reopen.

Chris, noticing that the hall was empty, took a careful and cautious step down towards the lab tech's lounge area. Not wanting to let his guard down, he would check behind himself with every other step.

So far everything was clear. He was finding it hard to hear the subtle moaning of the creatures with the loud banging of the elevator doors.

That was the very reason he never heard the creature lurking within the lounge area. Still, he was careful enough not to rush inside and stood farther back against the wall. The thing inside took notice of him before it had even turned around, almost as if it could smell him.

It started moaning louder and turned slowly, putting its arms out in front of it. Chris could see the blood soaked shirt and the cloudy white eyes. What he took most note of was the thing's jaw, which seemed to open and close in anticipation of the meal before it.

Chris started up the hall and saw that the creature was moving slowly and he knew he would have to take his time to lead it to the elevator.

"Come on poochie." Chris called after it as he backed away, never taking his eyes from the thing in front of him. He neared the corner and hot, rotten breath assaulted his face.

"Oh shit!" Chris yelled as he ducked quickly and scurried out of the thing's reach. He saw that the noise had drawn a few more of the undead out of hiding. Finding the path to the elevator clear, he ran as fast as possible towards it. He kicked his stool inside and hastily jumped onto it so that he could reach his safe spot.

Before he could pull himself up, a hand grabbed his ankle and started pulling him back down. More moans were mixing with the one that held him and Chris knew he had only a little amount of time to get to safety.

Chris kicked with all he had, and finally the thing let go. He swiveled into a position that let him see into the elevator and dropped his noose around the moaning zombie, which never stopped in its attempt to reach Chris.

Chris managed a small smile at his progress and got ready for the ride upstairs. As the doors began to close, a decaying hand reached inside and caused the doors to open again. Before the doors finally closed, Chris had three more of the shambling creature reaching up at him, ready to tear him to ribbons.

"Now isn't that just great." Chris said to himself as he held the rope like a leash. The elevator started to rise. "What the hell?" Chris asked. "I know I didn't push any buttons."

Jeff had suggested that they get a mirror from one of the bathrooms near the upstairs cafeteria. As they were walking across the upper levels, Jeff looked down into the lobby.

"What the hell was that?" He asked to no one in particular.

"What was what?" Janet asked as she looked for something below.

"Thought I saw something get on the elevator." Jeff said and immediately thought of Chris wandering the halls or waiting inside that office downstairs watching the monitors. The made it to the bathroom and after performing their standard check for zombies, which Jeff was sure he would still do out of habit even years from now, they carefully took the mirror from the wall.

"You ready to drop these things off in Levine's office?" Janet asked as Jeff lugged the mirror through the door.

"Ready when you are." Jeff replied shifting the weight of the mirror so that he could get a better grip.

"Lead the way." Janet said and stepped to the side to allow Jeff in front of her. "I've never been to that office."

The office of the late Mr. Levine was simple enough to find and once they unloaded their provisions into a corner of the room, Jeff turned to Janet and said, "Now all we need is to get the ropes from the lobby flagpoles and we can wrangle us up a zombie."

Janet shook her head at his attempt at humor, but she gave him a pity smile just the same. Then they were on their way.

Jeff entered the lobby and went to the flagpoles. He saw that one of them was broken and the ropes were already gone. "He wouldn't." Jeff said as he stood staring at the broken flagpole.

"Who wouldn't what?" Janet asked, but she gasped suddenly as she realized just what had happened.

"Why the hell would he do something like that?" Janet asked as she looked up at Jeff.

"Wants to prove he isn't useless." Jeff said as he started to go to the elevator. "And before you ask, yes he is that stupid." He kept a tight grip on the blade as he pushed the button to call the elevator.

"Come on. Come on." Jeff said as Janet walked up beside him.

"I'm sure he's fine." Janet said uncertainly.

Jeff said nothing, silently hoping that she was right. Then the bell dinged the arrival of the elevator and the doors opened. "Damn." That was all that Jeff had time to say before Hell was unleashed on the lobby.

Chris thought that this ride in the confines of his crawl space was one of the longest he had ever had. The constant noises and the rotten stench rising from the things below him were overpowering to say the least. He thought of nothing but how to get out of this situation.

Then the doors opened. The moaning roared louder and the things surged as one for the door. Chris then knew what had happened.

Janet stared in amazement when the doors opened. She had barely any time to react as the mass of things came right at them. She tried to reach for her gun, but found it was not on her. As one of the things put its cold, dead hands around her throat, she found enough breath to yell to Jeff that she had forgotten her gun in Levine's office and she saw the look on his face. It was not the disappointment she had expected, but one more along the lines of disbelief. But he was not looking at her. That was the last she saw as the thing proved to be too heavy and she fell over, the face of the thing drawing closer.

Jeff saw Janet fall and wanted for all he was worth to be able to reach her, but he had his own problems. He was trying to fight off two of the creatures that desperately wanted to snack on his tender vittles. Strangely and suddenly one of them had just flown back as if an invisible hand had smashed it in the chest. It landed hard against the back of the elevator and Jeff saw what had happened.

Chris more heard than saw the scene unfolding. Reacting as fast as he could, he pulled hard on the zombie he held with the rope. The rope went suddenly slack as the off balance creature came flailing backwards to land on the floor. Chris grabbed onto the rim of the hatch he was hiding in and, as he heard a familiar voice in terror, swung out to kick any of the creatures rushing at his friends. Screaming for all he was worth and sure that this was his last stand.

Jeff saw glimpses of what happened next. He saw Chris kick at the last standing creature and send it sprawling on the floor. "Get Janet!" Jeff yelled as he pushed back on his attacker. Jeff buried the blade into the skull of the thing and it fell for the final time.

Jeff saw Chris grab the thing on top of Janet and thrust it to the floor. Chris then drew back the pike he had made from the flagpole and he forced it through the things brain.

Without a pause, Chris pulled his weapon free and dispatched the undead he had just thrown to the floor. That left the one in the elevator.

Jeff stared in shock as Chris walked inside the elevator and bent down in front of the now rising zombie, careful to stay out of its reach. He saw Chris back up with something in his hand and Jeff realized that it was a rope.

"You actually did it huh?" Jeff said as Chris backed out with the zombie, careful to keep the creature out of reach by using the pike to force it back when it was too close.

"Well, I wanted a dog, but you know how messy they are to pick up after." Chris and Jeff both turned and marveled at Janet's comment. She stepped up behind Chris, put a hand on his shoulder and said softly, "Thanks."

"Not a problem." Chris said as he grinned at her.

"About earlier." Janet said as she backed up to give the guys room to maneuver their new pet to the stairs.

"Don't worry about it." Chris said as he started up the stairs, making sure that Jeff and Janet were behind him in case he tripped. "It's already forgotten."

They reached Levine's office without further incident. "Here's the thing. What do we do with him once we get him inside? I am damn sure he will not just sit quietly." Chris said trying his best to maintain control of the thing as it thrashed about always trying to get closer to them.

"We will just have to make him sit." Jeff said and ran inside the office only to return shortly with the chair from behind Levine's desk. Chris forced the thing back and it fell into Levine's chair. As it tried to stand, Chris would keep the pressure applied.

Chris handed the spear to Jeff and said, "You make sure he doesn't get up and I will wrap this rope around it." A few times around the chair and the length of the rope was spent. Chris had enough to stand just out of the thing's reach. "Now what? I let this go and he gets up."

"Give it here." Janet said as she reached for the rope. "I was in the Girl Scouts." She started to go behind the creatures and she could hear, but ignored Chris' whispered comment about not needing cookies. She ducked down at the back of the chair and was careful that the thing could not grab her. She tied the knots quickly and ran around to stand with Jeff.

"Let him go." Chris said and Jeff pulled the pike away. The thing struggled and tried to stand. It was held firmly. "Not bad." Chris admitted.

Chris took the pike and started pushing the chair into the room.

Jeff stood at the door as Chris put the thing behind Levine's desk. Chris walked over to him and said, "What's wrong with you? I haven't heard you say much since I got back."

"A couple of things." Jeff said. "First, we are almost out of here, so I am happy about that. And second," at this Jeff's voice fell to a whisper. "I have a date."

Chris looked shocked. He lowered his voice and said, "So which of the zombies finally said yes?"

"Bite me ass-gobbler. If you want, you can get a good sniff from the desk where your cleaning honey was."

"Touché." Chris said. "What do you say we finish this damn thing and get the hell out of here?"

"Works for me." Jeff said and they went to join Janet who was making the final preparations for the binding.

Chapter 16:

The Ties That Bind

The gang carefully maneuvered the captured zombie into the office and placed it in a large open space they had cleared out. The salt was poured in a circle around themselves and the seated creature. The candles were placed at the points specified on the list of instructions that Janet still held. The bowl was set on the floor and they sat next to it facing the zombie. Chris kept a tight grip on his spear just in case the thing got loose. They set the mirror up in front of them so that they could see themselves in it and laid the scalpel in front of it.

When all of these preparations were complete and each of them was seated as comfortably as they could be, Jeff asked, "Now what?"

Ascaroth waited impatiently for his pawns to complete their mission. He had made it simple enough. As tempted as he was to intervene, Ascaroth knew that too many ventures into that building would surely alert Cheitan to his presence. Time was running thin and he had to choose his moments carefully.

Ascaroth could almost feel the centering of the power and he knew that the group of people he had sought aid from had completed the circle. If all went well, he would be able to have Cheitan drawn from his sanctuary and they could perform one final act for him. After that, their fate was their own.

Again, Ascaroth sat down on the hard, craggy ground and closed his eyes. He sent himself out into the building to once again do his master's bidding.

Cheitan stood over the whimpering Alan Salvin practically feeding off of the despair and terror he sent out in waves. The last symbols had finally been drawn and he was ready to cement his place in history. All would know his name and they would tremble.

"Well Alan." Cheitan said as he stooped down to pick up Salvin. "It is time for you to leave us, but not to worry, your sacrifice will remake the world. I have spent these past years making you the perfect vessel and once I join my spirit with your flesh, I can no longer be forced back into the place that I came from. I will be bound here."

Cheitan put Salvin, who had long since abandoned any semblance of hope, onto the small chair he placed inside the center of his circle of symbols.

"Once we finish here, I can let my brothers out into the world to roam free and have all kinds of fun. Then this earth will be mine. And again I must thank you for your part in this. I have been preparing for this day for eons and now I can finally be free."

"Let's begin shall we?" Cheitan stood towering over Salvin, who sat still from shock, rocking back and forth slightly and staring into space with eyes that never seemed to focus on anything. He clapped his hands together once and darkness seemed to seep into the room. It flowed like liquid smoke, slowly inching towards Salvin and Cheitan.

Low guttural noises were coming from Cheitan as he knelt down to come face to face with Salvin. Nearly pressing their noses together, Cheitan continued his chant and the darkness drew nearer.

The room went suddenly cold. Goosebumps rose on their flesh and their breath could be seen. "Who turned on the AC?" Chris asked.

"Wasn't me." Jeff said, rubbing his arms in an effort to stay warm.

"Look." Janet said, pointing at the mirror they had in front of them. The silvered glass had fogged over and on it a message had appeared.

"Good work." It said and then the message was wiped clean only to be replaced with more fog. "Need blood of creature."

Again the message left and another showed itself, "In bowl."

Chris stood up and picked up the scalpel. "Hey Jeff. Hand me the bowl."

The bowl was given and Chris walked over to the securely tied thing, thinking to himself, *I hope she is as good at tying these knots as she thinks she is.*

Chris slowly and carefully crept up to the zombie, who had not once stopped trying to reach them. He drew a long cut across the creature's thrashing arm near the shoulder where it was most steady, but still far enough away from the mouth. The cut was deep enough that partially clotted blood flowed freely but the zombie gave no sign that it felt the pain from the cut.

The bowl was held as carefully as possible so that none of the gore splashed on Chris. When there was a good amount of the crimson liquid settling on the bottom of the bowl, he returned to the others, much to the dismay of the secured zombie. The bowl was placed in front of the mirror and again it fogged, "Must say words."

"If we have to say *Klatu verata nictu* that would kick major ass." Jeff said to Chris, who nodded his agreement.

A strange set of letters appeared on the mirror. A language that none of them knew was displayed before them.

"Well I sure hope that we don't have to be able to read this." Chris said as he stared at the seemingly gibberish phrase before him.

"Maybe if we just sound it out and get close enough." Jeff said as he tried to sound out the expression.

Janet started writing the words down in case they suddenly disappeared. When she finished, she turned to the guys and said. "Are you ready to get this done?"

They both nodded at her and she said, "Right. Let's do this."

Cheitan's face tightened with the effort it took to maintain his barriers and complete this last part of his plan. All that he would have to do is take over the body of this pathetic little man and nothing could force him back into The Pits.

Cheitan felt more strongly about never going back there than he had ever felt about anything. His eyes glowed with an unearthly orange glow as he leaned forward to within inches of Alan Salvin.

"Can you feel the power?" Cheitan practically screamed as winds whipped around the room. "We are nearly finished."

Cheitan reached for Alan so that the ritual could be completed, when suddenly a look of shock fell over Chietan as he stared at the scene before him.

"So this is the big bad huh?" Chris said as he stared at the figure frozen inside the circle. "Doesn't seem so tough now does he?"

Janet looked at Chris and said, "You do remember that he did make an entire building full of zombies right?"

Chris nodded and Jeff said, "How long do you think it will hold him?"

"Hopefully until we can get downstairs and mess up whatever he was working on." Chris said. "And why did I just let the bad guy know our plans? Isn't that their job to tell us what they were going to do?"

"You to need to get out more." Janet said. "Now let's get going before he gets out of there."

And with that they started to head back downstairs and into the basement. Deciding not to push their luck with the elevator, they take the stairs. The first flight still held the unmoving corpses of the former captain and the vice-president of Maverick Cosmetics.

Janet held a hand over her mouth and nose as she stepped over the rotting forms in a vain effort to save her senses from the strong odors. Chris walked a few paces ahead, silently hoping that they would blame it on the zombies.

As they rounded the next short flight of stairs, they heard the telltale moaning of the undead and the gang instantly went on the defensive. They had no desire to be caught unaware in these tight corridors. Janet stayed in front since she still had a precious few shots left in her pistol. Jeff and Chris stood behind in order to make sure that none of the things had come up from behind them through a door left open.

Janet leaned out over the railing and she could barely see the top of a balding, white head. Its skin had taken on a waxy look that you could almost see through. Even as unnerved as she was, Janet leaned farther over the edge and took aim as best as she could. The sound of the shot echoed loudly through the stairwell.

The thing fell quickly in a spray of blood and bone as the bullet tore through its skull. The gang took a few more cautious steps, remaining ever vigilant, and found that they could not hear anything.

"Of course," Chris complained. "That could be because I have no hearing left. Not that I am not grateful you understand. It is just that I would have liked to hear something sneaking around in here."

"Surprise, surprise," Jeff said. "Chris is complaining again. Ow!"

Jeff rubbed the spot on the back of his head where Chris had slapped him with the spike he carried. "Not to *complain* again, but I really think we need to pick up the pace here. Not sure how long that thing will hold him and I don't want to be around when he gets out."

"I agree." Janet said. "And if you two are done playing, we can get going any time." Janet turned and took the next flight of stairs.

They passed the door to the labs, and the next flight of stairs was thankfully zombie free. The group reached the final leg of their journey and before they had taken the first few steps of the last flight, Janet screamed. She pitched forward and tumbled hard down the stairs to land in a heap on the floor.

Her fall had happened so fast that she never even knew what hit her. Jeff saw it though and was yelling something to her. She couldn't really understand him. Everything seemed muffled to her. Then she saw him pointing under the stairs and there it was, a bloodstained hand was reaching through the gap between the stairs. She brought her gun up to fire and saw the guys scramble to get out of the way.

The undead creature started shuffling out from behind its hiding place under the stairs. She aimed, but her eyes were not focusing. She concentrated harder and fired off a shot that went wide. It was coming closer and she could see the guy's concern.

She tried another shot. This one clipped the shoulder of the thing. She was just too dazed from the fall. She felt herself yelling for them to help her, but she didn't really hear the words. She prayed that they heard her.

When the creature was only a few feet from her, it suddenly was jerked backwards. Jeff had grabbed it from behind and had thrown it against the nearby wall. Chris thrust the pike he held into its chest, pinning it in place. Chris ducked and Jeff drew the blade he held in both hands back like a baseball player swinging for the fences. The things head rolled off as Chris left the spear go and rolled to avoid the inevitable spraying of blood and gore.

She could see them gesturing wildly with their hands as they argued about something she could not quite make out. She saw Chris pull his weapon from the thing's chest as Jeff walked over to her.

She found that she could hear some of what he was saying and her mind was becoming less foggy. Apparently she hadn't injured herself as bad as she feared. Jeff reached a hand down to help her up and she stood a bit unsteadily for a minute gathering her senses.

Chris walked over and said something about her gun. She handed it to him and he ejected the clip, counting out the few remaining shells. There were five left as he replaced them and handed the gun back to her.

They looked concerned for her, but she waved it off and told them that she was getting better. They then went to the door to listen for anything on the other side.

The door opened into a steamy, hot hallway that ran in a straight line down the center of the floor. There were only two of the creatures lining the hall and they were at the far end.

"Want to make a bet that we have to go down there?" Chris said never taking his eyes off of the things before him.

"I say we just take care of them anyway. I would hate to walk out of one of these rooms and into their arms." Jeff said hefting his blade. They looked at Janet.

"Feeling better yet?" Jeff asked, concerned for her.

"I'm fine now." She lied. She wasn't ready at all in fact. She still felt a little dizzy, but she was determined to see this end as quickly as possible. She took a few cautious steps forward and when she didn't stumble or fall, she began feeling more confident.

"I think she should save as many shots as she can." Chris said. "Janet, if you take out one of them, me and Jeff can get the other."

She agreed to this plan and stepped closer in order to have a better shot. She took aim, fearing another miss and a wasted bullet. Her shot found its mark, but just barely as the back half of the things head exploded into tiny shards.

The lone zombie turned to face them. It stretched out its long arms and began a slow, methodical walk forward to try and reach the food waiting before it.

Chris ran a few steps and drew his arm back. His spear flew threw the air in a wobbling arc to bounce harmlessly off of the wall next to the thing. Jeff looked at him disapprovingly.

"You think you are in the Olympics or something?" Jeff asked as he looked at the discarded weapon.

"Dude, I was close OK." Chris replied feeling defensive about his missed throw.

"Now how are we gonna get close enough to him?" Jeff said pointing at the slowly advancing creature. "We were supposed to use your little stick to push it against the wall just like last time."

"Don't get your oversized panties in a bunch." Chris said flashing a grin at Jeff. "I have a Plan B." With that Chris set off at a run for the zombie.

"Moron." Jeff said as he took off after him.

Chris got closer to the undead thing and went into a kind of baseball slide, taking the legs out from underneath the approaching monster. As it fell, he continued to roll out of its way. Jeff arrived, nearly out of breath, and quickly dispatched it with a well-placed blow to the head.

Janet came running up behind him and said, "You two really need to seek some kind of counseling. You are so lucky that the thing didn't just fall on you."

"Luck has nothing to do with it." Chris said brushing himself off and picking up his poorly thrown weapon. "I have been killing zombies for years. Its all about the practice."

Chris walked over to examine the doors at that end of the hall.

Jeff said to him, "You do realize that video games do not really count as zombie killing experience?"

"Worked so far hasn't it? I am getting good at this." Chris asked shrugging his shoulders and turning to face one of the doors.

Janet walked up, stood beside Jeff and said, "He is the most egotistical person I have ever met."

"Or he's right." Jeff said as he walked over to Chris who was listening closely at one of the doors. "Anything?"

"I hear something, so just get ready." Chris said as he stepped back from the door, ready to throw it open and take care of any threats.

Janet came to stand in front of the door, her pistol ready in her hand. "On three." She said and began counting down.

"One." They tensed up and prepared themselves for whatever was inside. Chris gripped the handle even tighter and Jeff brought his blade back ready to swing at a moment's notice.

"Two." Janet continued. Sweat poured from Jeff as his adrenaline surged. He felt his heart pounding in his ears.

When the count hit three, Chris threw the door wide and Janet aimed a fast shot inside. Her senses had not completely returned so her shot was a little wide. They can be thankful that it was.

As Janet stared at the person sitting on the floor, she thought for sure she had brain damage. *It can't be,* she said to herself as she rubbed her eyes and looked again.

"Dude," Chris said nervously. "Why are we just standing here and not killing whatever was in there?"

Jeff shushed him with a glare, looked at Janet and said, "What's wrong?"

"Not sure." She said squinting at the seated figure. She walked into the room slowly, taking each step carefully in case she was attacked. She reached the seated figure and when it did not attack, but simply looked up at her with clear, but haunted eyes she said, "Mr. Salvin? Is that you?"

CHAPTER 17:

THE FATAL MISTAKE

Alan Salvin sat staring in disbelief at the group before him. They knelt down in front of him and one of them was firing questions at him that his mind just did not have the strength left to process. His mind managed to comprehend a few choice words and phrases and he began to understand just what they wanted from him. They wanted a way out.

Of course, he thought. *They need my code. Can't open the shutters without it.*

He concentrated hard on trying to remember his code that would open the gates. It seemed as though it was just out of reach, but if he could only think clearer, everything would come rushing back.

As he stared into the hopeful eyes of the girl kneeling before him, his fog that had been engulfing brain began to clear at last. He found that thoughts came much faster for him.

"I remember." Alan said suddenly.

"Dude, I think this guy is about done." Chris whispered to Jeff.

"Shh." Jeff said.

"Mr. Salvin," Janet said to him in a calm, soothing tone. "Are you alright?"

Alan Salvin sat up straighter and took hold of Janet's arm. The guys started forward, but she held them back with a wave from her free hand.

"The code." Salvin said concentrating hard on finding that one fact. "It's 12041952."

Janet's face brightened as she realized they were about to escape from this nightmare. She took a quick look back and noticed that the guys seemed more excited as well. They were grinning broadly and looking at the door, obviously anxious to leave.

"Come over here." Janet said. "Help me get him up. We can't just leave him here."

Chris and Jeff walked over to help Alan to his feet. Suddenly Chris put an arm across Jeff's chest to stop him. "Look." He said, pointing at the floor.

Scrawled in a strange red ink were symbols and a large circle drawn on the floor that, in the confusion of finding someone else alive, they had missed.

"They are his power." Salvin said unexpectedly, staring at the drawings on the floor. Alan did not bother to try and hide the fear he was feeling at simply looking at them. "He draws his energy from them."

"We have to get rid of these." Jeff said as he started looking around for something to start wiping up the markings. Chris helped him look while Janet tended to the slowly recovering Salvin.

"No good man." Chris said as he finished his search. "There is nothing in here we can use."

"On the way back here I saw a room marked 'Janitor'." Jeff said brightening. "Pretty sure that place would have something to clean this up with."

"Sounds like a good idea to me." Chris said and started walking for the door. He turned and asked, jerking his thumb in Salvin's direction, "What about him?"

"I'll stay and watch him." Janet said as she set herself down onto the floor.

"OK, but if anything strange happens, get to that office fast." Jeff said, concerned for her safety.

"I will." She said smiling, feeling happy at the worry that Jeff was showing for her.

"Fine. Kiss, kiss. Lovey crap." Chris said grabbing Jeff by the arm and dragging him towards the door. "Let's work on leaving this place now. You can make out later."

Jeff let himself be led outside saying, "You really are an ass."

"I know." Chris said as he shut the door.

Jeff walked beside Chris and felt the excitement that came with knowing that their ordeal was soon going to be over.

"So where do you think I should take her?" Jeff asked.

"What?" Chris said confused as to what he was talking about.

"Janet. On our date." Jeff said uneasily. "Where should we go?"

"Not that I don't care about your love life," Chris said. "But shouldn't we be worrying about the building full of things that want to eat us? Besides, just take her to some fast food place, but don't Super-Size anything. No woman on Earth is worth that. Here's the door."

Chris, still distracted from the conversation, opened the door without first listening to see if anything was inside. A tall figure in dirty, bloody coveralls lurched out at him, grabbing him around the throat.

Chris heard Jeff yell something. Then a faint whistle reached his ears as Jeff embedded his blade into the head of the clawing zombie.

"How many times have I done that for you now?" Jeff asked.

"Don't start with that crap again." Chris said coughing, rubbing his sore neck. He motioned for Jeff to go inside and Chris followed after him.

Lining the shelves were cleaning supplies of all kinds from the sort that you would find in nearly every home to the industrial strength that would surely get up the markings they needed to remove.

Chris reached for a gallon sized container on the middle shelf and said, "Hey, I think this one might even be strong enough to clean up after you."

"If it is that good, then bring it." Jeff said as he picked up a handful of cleaning towels. Together they left the janitor's office and went back to erase the symbols.

Janet was still sitting cross-legged on the floor. She stood up quickly and drew her pistol when she heard the door creak open. She quickly lowered her hand when she saw that it was only Chris and Jeff.

"That is the second time today you pointed that thing at me." Chris said grinning. "I think it is time you get those glasses checked."

He set the bucket of cleaner down and Jeff placed his bucket of water next to it.

"What's with the water?" Janet asked as she pointed at the bucket. "I don't plan on cleaning up after we are finished in here."

Jeff sighed and pointed at Chris. "We were halfway back before this illiterate bastard finally reads that the cleaner is a powder. I had to go all the way back and get some water."

Chris just shook his head and leaned over to open the bucket. "You haven't stopped complaining about that little walk ever since you got that water. It weighs what, five pounds?"

Chris dumped some of the powder into the water and saw it turn a sickly yellow color. "I would move if I were you guys." Chris said as he pointed to Janet and Salvin. He then picked up the bucket and poured the contents over the symbols on the floor.

Cheitan continued his relentless attempts to escape the feeble prison he found himself trapped inside of. *Where could they have learned such things? How could they do this to me?*

Cheitan began concentrating harder in an effort to break the barrier that held him to that particular spot.

"Will you shut up?" Cheitan screamed as he slammed a fist into the decaying face of the zombie seated next to him. Bone and blood scattered everywhere, lining the once pristinely cleaned office with gore.

The little outburst seemed to calm Cheitan down somewhat and with the noise of the moaning creature having finally ended; he found he was able to concentrate much better.

Cheitan started to gather his strength once more. He closed his eyes and drew upon the symbols of power he had grown so accustomed to. Suddenly his eyes shot open and he knew something had gone terribly wrong. He could no longer feel the power that the symbols brought him. It was as if they were being removed. Cheitan was preparing to redouble his efforts when something made him suddenly stop and stare at the small mirror before him.

"Having trouble?" the words appeared on the misted over mirror. Even though no sound could be heard, Cheitan could practically feel the arrogance and taunting in that phrase.

"Nothing I can't handle. Do you really believe that they can hold me here?" Cheitan said with a confidence he was not so sure he felt.

"Almost done." The words came again, "Destroy your power."

Cheitan was becoming angry and he found that he wanted to just crush the taunting mirror and whoever was sending the messages.

"Foolish plan failed." Again the mirror revealed its message.

Cheitan was practically seething with fury as the messages continued their humiliating taunts. Without even realizing what was happening, Cheitan was growing stronger. The bonds that held him in place were growing weaker.

When he finally reached for the small rectangle of silvered glass that had been torturing him, Cheitan found the movements effortless. As he brought the mirror down to shatter on the hard corner of a desk, Cheitan had calmed enough to realize what had happened. He was free.

Jeff and Chris were kneeling down scrubbing their hardest in an attempt to remove the symbols painted on the floor.

"And you said being a security guard wasn't glamorous." Jeff said as he went to work on another image.

"It does have its perks." Chris replied as he sat up straighter throwing his towel to the floor and using the back of his hand to wipe the sweat from his face. "So how much of this stuff do we actually have to get up anyway?"

"Well the last time I did this." Jeff began and put a hand on his chin as though in deep thought. "Wait a minute, I have never done this! So how the hell would I know how much to get up. I say we might as well get rid of it all."

"Man you get snippy when you have to do manual labor." Chris said as he went back to work scrubbing the markings. "You think that Salvin guy is ok? Seems a bit flaky."

"As long as…" Jeff started to say, but would not get the chance to finish.

The door flew in off of its hinges, shattered wood pelting the gang with sharp projectiles. A large figure stood menacingly in the doorway. Anger came off of him in waves.

"Guess they don't make barriers like they used to." Chris said as he scrambled to his feet, grabbing for the seemingly small pike he held in his left hand.

Janet ran up beside them as they stared at Cheitan.

"Did you fools really think you could hold me?" Cheitan was livid with rage, his body shaking with the pent up anger. "I will have my day and there is nothing a few pathetic pieces of shit like you can do about it!"

Cheitan started walking forward, slowly and methodically, enjoying the fear that he felt from the three interlopers. He would no longer tolerate their presence. It was time to end this little game.

Janet stared in shock, barely hearing the shouting next to her. She was certain that this was her last stand. Death had come for them. She snapped back into reality as a hand grabbed her shoulder, shouting at her to do something.

"Dammit woman, shoot him!" Chris shouted at her. She finally remembered the gun in her hand and fired off a few rounds that went extremely wide.

"Nice shooting Tex." Chris said as he bounced on the balls of his feet. He took a precious second to look at Jeff and said, "While I have him distracted, you get everyone to the office."

Before Jeff could even reply, Chris ran forward to meet Cheitan.

Jeff was forced to duck as Chris came flying back over his head to land in a heap on the cold cement floor.

Jeff and Janet backed over to Chris to make sure he was still breathing. Jeff, never taking his eyes off of the advancing Cheitan, gave a casual kick to Chris to rouse him from his sleep.

"No time for sleeping." Jeff said as Chris sat up.

"Did we win?" Chris asked rubbing his head and rising gingerly to his feet.

"Nope."

Cheitan was upon them, his eyes glowing with the energy his hatred for the three before him fueled. As he reached down to finally smite the troublesome pests, he felt something land on his back.

"You cannot stop me!" Cheitan roared as he reached around his back grabbing the flailing person. Cheitan, so livid with fury that he did not see the consequences of his actions, threw the struggling form against the nearest wall where it landed with a loud snap. Cheitan turned and all thoughts of crushing the group before him had left. On the floor, obviously dead by the odd angle of his neck and the cold unseeing eyes, was Alan Salvin.

Cheitan looked down at the result of his outburst and wailed in anger. Sparks of power crackling around his body. Surely he would make them pay slowly. Cheitan prepared himself for the days of fun he would have ruining their bodies and looked into the corner that they had been huddling in. They were gone.

CHAPTER 18:

ESCAPE

Chris, Jeff and Janet stood transfixed in the small corner of the room, all of them were sure that the next moment would be the last they would spend on this Earth. They could not believe the unlikely event unfolding before them. Janet, who had been keeping an eye on him, saw Salvin slowly rise from the floor where he was sitting. Her mind was so wracked with fear that she could not quite understand what was happening.

She saw Salvin as he ran up behind Cheitan and leapt onto his back. She stared wide-eyed in horror as Cheitan threw him against the wall and he crumbled to the floor with a sickeningly wet smack, obviously dead.

Jeff immediately saw the opportunity for their salvation and grabbed a hold of Chris and Janet pulling them forward. Together they ran for the doorway and began their race up the stairs and to their freedom.

"Why did he do that?" Janet asked as they rounded the first flight, panting from the fast pace.

"Not sure." Jeff said as he took hold of a handrail and bounded around the corner. "You have to give the guy credit for having a large set of balls though."

"Let's get out of here first." Chris said as he reached for the handle of the door that would lead them into the laboratory hall. "We can marvel over his testicular fortitude later!"

They sped around the corner and Chris nearly slipped on the mess of zombie blood. Jeff caught his arm and they went inside Salvin's office, ready to use the final gift Salvin had given them to get away from this nightmare.

Chris reached the small opening near the back of the room that held the switches for the steel security gates. "Janet." He said as he pointed in the direction of the front of the room. "I need you to go and keep an eye on those monitors. I want to know when that big bastard is coming."

"Don't you mean 'if'?" Janet asked as she turned to take up her position on monitor duty.

"Would you just let us live if we did those things to you?" Jeff asked. He looked into Janet's face and he saw the realization dawn on her. The only way they were going to make it out alive was if that code was genuine.

He reached for the keyboard resting on the small shelf and started to enter the code. He entered the first digit and was about to continue entering the rest, when he stopped unexpectedly. He stared at the screen and his head fell forward.

"What the fuck are you waiting for Chris?" Jeff asked practically screaming his question.

Chris turned and looked at him, an uneasy feeling welling up inside of him. He tried to speak, but he was not sure how he could explain what he was thinking.

"You have those gates open yet?" Janet yelled hopefully from the front of the room where she was bathed in the soft glow of the monitors' light.

"We can't leave." Chris whispered. He looked into the confused face of Jeff as Janet came running back to them.

"What the fuck do you mean, 'We can't'?" Janet asked, grabbing Chris by the shoulders and shaking him hard.

"Listen." Chris said as he put his hands up in a defensive posture. "I want to get out of this shit hole as much as anyone, but we can't open those gates."

Jeff looked as if he were about to just knock Chris out and enter the code himself when he finally understood just what Chris was talking about.

"I never thought I would be saying this, but he's right." Jeff said somberly and he stepped away from the console wringing his hands in frustration.

"Have you both gone completely insane?" Janet screamed. She ran back to the console and made to reach for the keyboard. Jeff grabbed her around the waist and pulled her away.

"Let go of me now!" Janet said, struggling helplessly in his grip. "We have to leave."

"Janet just calm down." Jeff said as he turned her around so that he could look into her eyes. "Just let us explain."

She stopped fighting him for the moment and stood there with her arms crossed. "This had better be good."

"Janet." Chris said as calmly as he could. "You have to understand that if we open those gates, any of those zombies still wandering around could get out."

"Exactly." Jeff said as he picked up where Chris left off. "And if they escape, they could hurt and infect more people. Then it is not just a building full of them, it will be a city. Eventually more."

Janet let her shoulders slump, as she finally understood what had caused them to delay their freedom. They were right and she knew it. Those gates had to remain closed until the creatures were dealt with.

"Fine." That was all she said as she resigned herself to her fate. For lack of anything else to do she went back to stand watch at the security monitors.

"Jeff! Chris! Get over here!" Her tone was so urgent that the guys wasted no time in getting to her. What they saw in those monitors was something they would not have expected.

Looking into one of the monitors that showed a long view of the hall running along the labs, they saw Cheitan emerge forcefully from the door. He started walking with a purpose right for them, when he just stopped.

A small man walked up to him, no fear showed in the confident strides he took. It was clear that the two were talking, but no one inside Salvin's office could hear the conversation. It was Janet who decided to take action. She walked over to the large double doors and opened one slightly, straining her ears, listening for any sounds.

Cheitan bellowed his frustration. His scream of anguish could be felt reverberating throughout the entire building. The sudden realization of what he had just done washed over him. He had killed the one he had been preparing for many years.

Cheitan stared down at the broken, battered corpse of Alan Salvin. His eyes glowed with power. Eldritch power crackled from his fingertips. He turned and left the room that had been his one true place of peace in this entire plane. Such was his anger that his every step left small cracks in the floor.

Cheitan could feel their presence as they huddled in the dark office. A smile crossed his face as he thought of the pain he was about to inflict. He trudged up the stairs preparing to disembowel the fools who had sought to thwart him. *Somehow they tricked me. They made me kill him. They ruined my dream.*

These thoughts echoed in his mind as he crushed the handle to the door and tore it from the hinges. As he took his first steps into the hall, he stopped and glared at the smug face coming towards him.

"Hello again Cheitan."

"Ascaroth." Cheitan spat the name out like it was poison. "How can you be here? My wards should have kept the likes of you from ever stepping foot in here."

"They had." Ascaroth started as he took a few confident steps forward. "At least until my little pawns took care of your barrier."

"I had a feeling that someone was helping them." Cheitan said as he stared into the eyes of Ascaroth, wanting nothing more than to tear the head from his body. "They could not have bound the likes of me without help."

"That was quite an ingenious idea." Ascaroth chuckled. "Not really my idea, but the result was worth it just to see the look on your face. Priceless." Ascaroth leaned casually against the wall. "Your little plan has failed."

"I still have a chance." Cheitan interrupted, taking a few menacing steps forward. "There are still ways to finish this."

"I wanted to tell you something." Ascaroth could not hide the pure elation he took in the defeat of Cheitan. "Your friends, their probably already dead. The master was not happy when he found out what you were planning."

"Do you really think that I care what that coward thinks?" Cheitan screamed. "No longer will I have to bend to his will. This world will bend to mine!"

Ascaroth actually laughed. He stood and stepped closer to Cheitan. "You are already finished. Your punishment will be legendary. And it was all thanks to a few meddling humans." Ascaroth threw his head back and laughed harder. His joy stopped suddenly as he stared at the nearly impossible sight.

Cheitan's face was mere inches from his own. Cheitan allowed his eyes to fall downwards and Ascaroth's gaze followed Cheitan's. There, where only the center of his chest should be, stuck the end of Cheitan's arm and when he withdrew that, blood flowed freely onto the carpeted floor.

Ascaroth gasped and dropped to his knees. Cheitan knelt down beside him, "Where is your arrogance now?" A laugh that was devoid of any mirth erupted from Cheitan.

"My dream will still come to pass and you can go back to Hell knowing that you could not stop me. I will rebuild the symbols. I will choose another vessel." With a flourish, Cheitan turned and stalked back down the stairs, all thoughts of those hidden in Salvin's office temporarily forgotten. He turned once to watch the life's blood pour out of Ascaroth before finally continuing to his sanctuary.

Janet, Jeff and Chris heard the conversation happening at the end of their small hallway. They learned more than they had ever thought, like the name of their mysterious benefactor.

"See, told you he was evil." Chris whispered triumphantly. Then they also heard the wet snapping sound as Cheitan pushed his hand through the chest of Ascaroth. A collective gasp escaped them as they each realized their one source of help in this freak show was lying on the floor, dying.

They waited carefully as Cheitan departed, ever afraid that he would just turn around and come after them. Killing them slowly.

When nothing happened and they were sure that Cheitan had gone, Chris took a tentative step outside the room they used to think was safe. They quickly raced around the corner at the end of the hall and found their benefactor lying in a pool of his own blood.

Jeff bent low in order to get a better look at the one called Ascaroth. As he crouched down low, Ascaroth reached a hand forward, grabbing Jeff's shirt. Jeff was pulled in close as Chris and Janet came up on either side of Ascaroth.

Janet, worry displayed in her voice, said, "Is there anything we can do?"

Ascaroth looked at her and then back down at his chest and said, "Does it really look like there is something you can do? I don't have much time and there are things I need to tell you."

Ascaroth strained and grunted through the spasms of pain that wracked what was left of his body. He could feel himself dying. He knew he had to tell them everything and quickly.

Janet spoke up again asking, "What is all of this? What is going on?"

Ascaroth did not bother to hide his annoyance, after all, he only had a short time left and he could not be bothered to answer any and all questions thrown at him.

Ascaroth reached inside the pocket of his long overcoat and pulled out a small glass vial. It had a strange silvery glow about it.

"What the hell is that?" Chris asked trying to get a closer look.

"This, impetuous one, is what you will need to finally defeat Cheitan." Ascaroth continued his tale, "In this vial is the only known substance that can kill one of us permanently."

"Seems like a big hole in the chest is helping you along with that whole death thing." Jeff commented.

"So it would to someone with a limited amount of intelligence. You see, I cannot truly die in your simple terms." Ascaroth pushed his back against the wall to better support himself, blood running down the once neatly cleaned wall. "When I die here, I will simply be transported back to where I came from. Now, time is almost up for me and if you do not keep quiet I will make sure to have you sent to me when you die."

Chris and Jeff gulped down their next few comments, allowing the fading Ascaroth to finish his story.

"This vial contains the blood of an angel." There was a collective gasp from the three people in front of Ascaroth, but none dared interrupt this time. "The blood came from one of the angels who fought against my master during the Great War. My master knew that such an item would inevitably prove invaluable so he had it hidden where none but he would be able to reach it."

The group continued to stare at the strange liquid in utter fascination. Ascaroth went ahead with the rest of his story.

"You must take this and mix it with the Philosopher's Stone. It is a chemical mixture I overheard Cheitan mention on more than one occasion. That is what caused all of this." His breath was coming in short, ragged gasps as he summoned all of his willpower to continue. "Cheitan managed to use that mixture to bond the essence of demons to the bodies of humans. Likewise this mixture should allow the essence of the angel to bond with Cheitan and that should kill him."

"So let me see if I get this straight." Chris said and saw the frustrated look on Ascaroth's face. "Somehow this Cheitan guy that has been trying to kill us, and damn near succeeded, created zombies by mixing their blood…"

"Not just their blood you simpleton." Ascaroth said angrily. "Their very essence. What you would call the soul."

"OK then." Chris said making a mental note to choose his words more carefully. "He bonded their essence to a human and that turned them into zombies."

"Of a sort." Ascaroth said growing ever impatient. "He plans to use these infected people to spread his army. For each one of those infected with the essence of the demon can spread a little piece of it to others. Eventually there would be none of you left. You see, he does not just want to kill and torture, if that were all he wanted, he never would have left. No, he wants to rule this place. To make Hell on Earth."

Chris continued. "And we are supposed to take this vial, which is angel's blood no less, and mix it with some chemicals and somehow get it into his bloodstream. Am I getting all of this right?"

"For once you are correct." Ascaroth said, his head dropping to one side. "My time here is up. Maybe I will see you all again one day."

"If it's all the same to you." Jeff said still trying to grasp this latest conversation. "I would rather we didn't."

"Farewell." Ascaroth said and faded into nothingness.

Chris, Jeff and Janet stood and stared for a moment at the smear of blood streaking the wall. "Well that sure was interesting." Jeff said finally as he took notice that Janet had not said a word in some time. "Something wrong Janet?"

"I am just trying to wrap my head around this." She said still not focusing on the guys, her gaze not leaving the wall.

"We really should get going." Jeff said as he turned her away from the scene. "We still have to find this Philosopher's Stone and mix this stuff with it." He stared at the glowing vial for another few seconds, hardly able to believe that he was holding the blood of an angel, when he always considered himself an atheist.

"Guess it's time to re-think that whole afterlife thing, huh?" Chris said clapping a hand on his shoulder.

"I guess." It was all Jeff could manage to say.

"So where do you think we can find this Stone?" Chris asked Janet in an obvious attempt to get her attention focused on the task at hand.

"Only one place would have it." She said confidently. "Faustus' lab. That was where this all started I believe and it should end there."

"Seems like we should be going then." Jeff said as he lowered the vial.

After a few more moments, the group turned as one and headed into Faustus' lab. Janet having already taken note of some of the items in this room felt confident that she could find the needed chemical mixture rather quickly.

Cheitan sat once more upon the cold stone floor, retracing the symbols that had been removed by the foolish interlopers. His vessel, the one to which he planned on bestowing the blessing of his own essence, was lying broken and bloodied on the floor. Cheitan knew he had nearly ruined his own plans. Nearly.

There were others still alive in this building and while they were not groomed to be perfect for him, well, any port in a storm. He would need one of them and soon. Before Ascaroth made it back home and brought others.

The circle was nearly complete and the symbols had been recreated. He began to feel his strength returning. That was when he felt something wrong.

There was activity in the lab. "I have had enough of their interference. It is time I ended this." With that, Cheitan rose. His body glowed with returned power and he marched off to end the miserable existence of the three annoyances.

Janet searched the lab as fast as she could, the gravity of their situation weighing upon all of them. She knew she was the only one who could prepare the mixture, so she felt the extra pressure that came along with that responsibility.

In one of the larger cabinets she found a wide assortment of containers. There on the top shelf was the one she sought. She brought it down and set it on one of the countertops in the lab. Then she grabbed a large glass container and began to pour the Philosopher's Stone inside of it.

When she felt she had a sufficient amount, no exact measurements were given to her. She added the silvery liquid to the mixture. She saw no true reaction, and in truth she was not sure that she expected one.

"Dude." Chris said quietly. "Is it just me or are you feeling exceptionally useless right about now?"

"Not just you man." Jeff replied equally as quiet. "But what can we do? She is the expert in all of this. We just have to wait for her to finish. Then we can get out of here."

"We still have the problem of the rest of those things getting out once we open the gates." Chris said.

"How about we deal with the larger thing trying to kill us first." Jeff said. "Then we can worry about them. Besides, I think that killing the big guy might just kill all of the zombies."

"You really think so?" Chris asked skeptically.

"Worked in the movies." Jeff said.

"Good enough for me." Chris replied.

"There!" Janet exclaimed. "Finished. Now all I have to do is get some of it into this syringe and you guys can inject Cheitan with it."

"You know Jeff." Chris said mockingly. "It is all equal treatment until it comes down to killing some big bad monster. Then it is all, 'Let the men do it!'"

"Downright sexist if you ask me." Jeff replied with a smile.

"I guess we just have to…" Chris started to say.

"Have to what?" a deep booming voice asked as the door to the lab was blown inwards.

"Bloody hell." Chris said in disbelief.

"That is my plan, yes." Cheitan smiled.

A still calm came over the room as Janet, Jeff and Chris stared at the powerful figure before them. They could not see how they stood a chance at defeating this creature.

All of a sudden Jeff raced forward with Chris close behind. Jeff brought up his blade and struck with all he was worth. Cheitan caught his arm in a bone-crushing grip and tossed him effortlessly backwards to land among the overturned tables.

Chris tried to keep his distance, all the while hoping to buy time for Janet to complete the serum. He thrust out with his pike at any opening Cheitan would give him. The fight was short lived as Cheitan grabbed one end of the spear and pulled Chris into him. Cheitan immediately wrapped one of his large hands around Chris' throat.

Come on Janet. Chris thought hopefully. *Get that shit finished.* Chris could not draw a breath as he was suspended from the floor like a rag doll. Chris barely heard Jeff untangle himself from the massive wreckage of tables and chairs. Black spots were beginning to swim before his eyes as the oxygen in his body was running thin. Unconsciousness was moments away.

Cheitan drew Chris up so close that Chris looked right into those cold snakelike eyes. Chris never felt the impact as Jeff threw himself at Cheitan. That gamble had not paid off like they had hoped. Now Jeff was being held as well.

Cheitan marveled at the sheer persistence of these pathetic creatures. To throw themselves at him so recklessly would only invite death. Only one of them had the intelligence to stay clear of him. He would save her for last. Let her watch her friends die slowly.

Cheitan carried the two former guards over to the large viewing window facing the hall and pushed them up against it. He held them off of the floor, allowing their feet to dangle in midair. He was relishing in the pale shade of blue that their faces were becoming. He reveled in their deaths. They who had caused him so much pain and time would be made to suffer. Their deaths would take hours.

Janet watched in horror as her friends were being killed in front of her. She had forgotten all about her mission. She could only stop and stare as they were carried over to the window. That was when she had decided.

Cheitan was taunting Chris and Jeff as they hung there. He was telling them of the many ways he was going to torture them before he allowed them to die. Then he was screaming. Cheitan felt a deep pain the likes of which he had not known existed.

He dropped those he was holding, all thoughts of killing them temporarily forgotten, and reached around behind his back to grab something that burned like all the fires of Hell never had.

It was a small needle. Chetain stared at it in puzzlement. Then he took notice of the faint silvery traces left inside the tube. Then he saw her and he knew she was responsible.

The guys were slowly recovering, doing everything they could to get to their feet once they realized what was happening.Surely this had to be a lie.

Jeff screamed an inhuman roar and ran right for Chetian as he sank his impossibly long teeth into the soft throat of Janet. Jeff had barely reached Cheitan when he was slapped back to fall against the cement wall.

Jeff rose again, but a hand gripped his wrist and spun him around. "We have to go!" Chris said hurriedly.

"He's killing her!" Jeff screamed as he tried to shake off Chris' grip.

Chris looked into his friend's eyes and said, "She is already gone. There is nothing we can do for her. We have to leave."

With hate filling his eyes, Jeff looked back at the monster that had killed Janet. He saw the thing just drop her to the floor like she was nothing. And then it came for them. Jeff took a last look at the unmoving form of Janet and left the room, knowing he could never forgive himself for leaving her there. For letting her die.

Cheitan watched as they ran from the room. He laughed as the blood of the woman coated his tounge. Even as he fell to his knees, weakened beyond anything he had ever felt, he laughed.

Jeff and Chris reached Salvin's office and entered the code for the control panel for the gates.

"Jeff." Chris said as he took a moment to gather his thoughts. "I am sorry about what happened in there."

"Just drop it." Jeff growled.

"I'm just trying to say…" Chris tried to explain.

"I said drop it!" Jeff screamed and shoved Chris backwards. Chris slipped on something lying on the floor. He reached down to throw it and almost laughed, if it wouldn't have seemed inappropriate. It was a small .38 caliber handgun.

Jeff looked at what Chris had found and while the anger was still there, Chris was certain it was not meant towards him. Jeff just nodded and they headed for the stairs.

Sparing one last glance in the lab, they saw that Cheitan had not moved. He was lying on the floor next to Janet. Chris looked at Jeff and handed him the gun.

Jeff emptied every round into the still form of Cheitan. The body didn't move once. "Looks like you did it." Jeff said to the woman he cared for. "You beat him after all."

"I have an idea." Chris said as he looked into Jeff's watering eyes. "We will not just leave her here next to that fucking thing! We are taking her with us."

Jeff nodded and almost smiled at his friend as they carefully stepped around the form of Cheitan to retrieve the body of Janet.

They start walking up the last flights of stairs when the building shook again.

Cheitan was brought back into awareness when sudden pain wracked his body. He felt the rounds penetrate his skin but he could do nothing to stop them. He was paralyzed. He felt himself slipping away. With the last of his energy, he would make sure that none escaped his domain alive. Again he sent out the power in waves that rocked the entire structure down to its foundation.

Then Cheitan collapsed.

Outside of Maverick Cosmetics there were news vans and reporters from the local stations lining the front lawn. All of them were staring at the strange steel coverings that had come down over the windows. No one could reach anyone on the inside. Communication with the people inside was cut off.

For the last three hours they had reported the situation, having been first alerted when one of the guards had tried to return for his lunch can and had found the building sealed.

"So Mr. Richards." The news reporter from Channel 16 began.

"Just call me Mike."

"So Mike." She continued. "What did you see here tonight?"

"Well." Mike started to explain as he placed his sandwich in his other hand. "It was the end of my shift and these two imbeciles were…"

"Just a minute." The reporter said. "The shutters are rising. Jimmy, get a shot of this." She pointed at the large double doors that were placed at the front of the building. "Someone is coming."

"I'll handle this." Mike said as he reached for his spare set of keys to the front doors. He swung them wide once he realized whom it was. "Hey it's you!" Mike smiled warmly at the figure approaching him. He walked up and offered his coat.

"What the hell happened in there Ja…" His seeming kindness was cut short as a set of sharp teeth ripped into his forearm, tearing away a large piece of flesh.

"What the hell is wrong with you Janet?" Mike yelled as he backed away.

The reporters closed in on her. They tried to get her on camera. They tried to ask her questions.

EPILOGUE:

WAR

Six months later.

The walls were cold and utilitarian. Everything was in order. A group of men sat in a darkened room waiting on one other. They never heard him arrive outside the building. They were in too deep to hear anything from the outside.

The door opened and the soft hallway light seeped into the room. The man took his rightful place at the head of the table. His briefcase was opened on the table and he removed a large stack of file folders and a videocassette tape.

"Gentlemen." He said addressing the people seated around him. "What you are about to see is footage of Patient Zero."

He placed the tape in the VCR and hit play. On screen there was the Channel 16 logo and the building that had once belonged to Maverick Cosmetics. Now it was theirs. The assembled grouping of men saw the attacks first hand. They marveled at the ferocity and were repulsed by the carnage.

An older man leaned forward once the footage was complete and the room was filled with soft light. "As all of you may know, Patient Zero was not the only one recovered from the site. In fact the first report we received of this incident came from the only survivors. They managed to get this footage and it came into our hands."

Another man spoke up, "But too much time has passed. By now the disease has spread farther then we could have imagined. We have our top scientists working with Patient Zero to find a cure. Until that day, we have sent special ops teams to deal with this ever growing threat."

"And the public still has no real knowledge?" Asked the man seated at the head of the table.

"Of course not sir." Another replied.

"And where are the two that brought this to our attention?"

"They are currently hunting with Team Omega in Canada."

"And the cure?"

"Nothing yet sir." A small man said. "Progress is slow, but my team is confident that results will be had by the end of the year."

"Until then." The head officer said. "We must keep this contained."

"Yes Sir." The assembled soldiers said in unison.

Deep in the depths of the same building was a lone cell. Darkness filled the room, but the one inside did not fear the dark.

They thought they beat me. But I will prevail. I will become whole again! I will escape. I will feed! An insane laughter reverberated through the dank, empty halls.